SPECIAL MESSAGE TO READERS

This book is published under the auspices of

THE ULVERSCROFT FOUNDATION

(registered charity No. 264873 UK)

Established in 1972 to provide funds for research, diagnosis and treatment of eye diseases. Examples of contributions made are: —

A new Children's Assessment Unit at Moorfield's Hospital, London.

•

Twin operating theatres at the Western Ophthalmic Hospital, London.

•

A Chair of Ophthalmology at the University of Leicester.

•

The establishment of a Royal Australian College of Ophthalmologists "Fellowship".

You can help further the work of the Foundation by making a donation or leaving a legacy. Every contribution, no matter how small, is received with gratitude. Please write for details to:

THE ULVERSCROFT FOUNDATION,
The Green, Bradgate Road, Anstey,
Leicester LE7 7FU, England.
Telephone: (0116) 236 4325

In Australia write to:
THE ULVERSCROFT FOUNDATION,
c/o The Royal Australian College of Ophthalmologists,
27, Commonwealth Street, Sydney,
N.S.W. 2010.

Love is
a time of enchantment:
in it all days are fair and all fields
green. Youth is blest by it,
old age made benign:
the eyes of love see
roses blooming in December,
and sunshine through rain. Verily
is the time of true-love
a time of enchantment — and
Oh! how eager is woman
to be bewitched!

THE CONTRACTED MARRIAGE

Returning to England in the wake of Charles II, Stephen Ansell finds homecoming no cause for jubilation, for, in common with many other Royalist families, he faces ruin. Forced to humble his pride and ask his ex-Roundhead uncle for help, he travels to Norfolk. His aunt and cousins promptly advise him to marry an heiress, and set about trying to achieve this. Stephen does fall in love, but not with the rich and charming Lucy . . .

JOAN NORTON

THE CONTRACTED MARRIAGE

Complete and Unabridged

ULVERSCROFT
Leicester

First published in Great Britain in 1980 by
Robert Hale Limited
London

First Large Print Edition
published September 1994
by arrangement with
Robert Hale Limited
London

British Library CIP Data

Norton, Joan
The contracted marriage.—Large print ed.—
Ulverscroft large print series: romance
I. Title
823.914 [F]

ISBN 0–7089–3154–5

Published by
F. A. Thorpe (Publishing) Ltd.
Anstey, Leicestershire

Set by Words & Graphics Ltd.
Anstey, Leicestershire
Printed and bound in Great Britain by
T. J. Press (Padstow) Ltd., Padstow, Cornwall

This book is printed on acid-free paper

For
Mum and Lee

1

A LENGTHY shadow jogged at his side as Stephen Ansell rode the last few miles of the long journey that had taken him from his home in Cheshire to London and on into Norfolk. Since leaving King's Lynn he had ridden in a daze of fatigue but when another horse and rider moved out from under some trees he jerked out of his reverie.

"Are you the new Commissioner of Sewers?"

Stephen was instantly alert. It was the second time in the space of little more than an hour he had been asked that. In the King's Lynn market-place, where he had stopped to ask the way, he had been struck by the atmosphere of sullen animosity of the groups of men standing about watching him. Someone had asked the same question and it was not until he had given assurance that he was only a passing traveller that he had been directed and wished godspeed.

This time there was no animosity. Nor was there warmth. The man reached the open centre of the track and Stephen could see that he was a big brute — both tall and burly. His hair was short-cropped in the Puritan style and his clothes plain and sober. A steward or upper servant, Stephen guessed.

Aloud he said: "No, I'm not the Commissioner of Sewers. I would find Banks House — can you give me the way?"

The man stared at him a moment, then pointed to a left-hand fork in the track.

"Along there. Some half mile." Abruptly he turned his horse and rode away into the gloom.

Stephen started along the lower track. With the setting of the sun the air had turned damp and the smell of decay was sharp in his nostrils. It had been a warm day but now wisps of mist were rising above the clumps of dank grass and reeds. Beyond the marsh was the sea but in the misty half-light it was impossible to tell where the marsh ended and the sea began.

I should have stayed at sea, Stephen

thought bitterly. If I had remained there I shouldn't be in this position. No, that wasn't strictly true, he acknowledged he would have had to return home sometime.

The predicament he was in was only too common during that early part of the Restoration — that of the Royalist returning home to find his estate depleted by Parliamentary fines and taxes, and the young King, however grateful he might be, totally without means to make reimbursement. Stephen's case was aggravated by a split in family loyalties and by his own pride.

Even now, fifteen years later, he could still feel the anguish and disbelief he had experienced when, after the Battle of Naseby and the death of his father, his mother had told him that they could not turn to Uncle William for help as William was for Parliament. Instead they would go to France. His father's sister, Bess, had been his favourite aunt and there had been deep affection between her husband, William Perrington, and the young Stephen. The defection of his uncle had been almost as deep a hurt as the death of his father and the pain had lasted throughout the years of exile.

When Stephen returned to England in the wake of the new King, Mr Perrington had written to him offering help and financial aid. Stephen, still at Court and full of jubilation at being advanced from a baronet to a baron, plus a purse from the King of £100, had ignored the letter and the offer of friendship.

The jubilation had not lasted long once he did go home. One look round Deeford showed him nothing but desolation and neglect. The house, after the initial billeting of troops, had been left empty and rotting for the rest of the Commonwealth period. All over the estate stock and rents had been rigorously seized until his tenants could hardly feed themselves. The only consolation was that the estate was complete. So many Royalists had been obliged to sell all or part of their estates to raise funds or to pay taxes and for them there was no recompense.

Stephen began the gigantic task of the restoration of Deeford with energy bred of enraged dismay. Even the time of the year was against him. It was mid autumn and he was racing against shortening hours of daylight and increasingly bad weather but if he left matters as they were until spring he would miss another whole season. If only he had not wasted weeks dallying in London or bought any new clothes. His tastes were not extravagant but he wished he had kept the few guineas he had spent.

The King's £100 was vanishing at an alarming rate. Working with the men he managed to stir out of their lethargy, Stephen made his largest barn weatherproof and repaired the roof of his own house and those of several of his tenants. He also purchased two cows and a work-horse but there his resourses ended. He realised that if he was to purchase the seed and cattle he needed to bring back his lands to full productivity without selling off part of his estate or borrowing from a money-lender at an exorbitant interest rate he would have to apply to his uncle for a substantial loan.

Mr Perrington was willing to supply this it seemed — and he could also give the expert advice Stephen needed. William Perrington, the younger son of an earl, had owned a fair-sized estate at the start of the war and, being on the side of Parliament, would have lost little of his wealth. His offer proved this.

For a few days Stephen had procrastinated but finally he had smothered his pride and, leaving his steward to carry on as best he could with the improvements that could be afforded, had set off for London only to find that his uncle and aunt were in Norfolk seeing to the affairs of their wards, the young Earl of Gerton and his sister.

Spending an evening with a friend before continuing his journey, Stephen had gleaned a few facts about his cousins by marriage. The boy had succeeded to the title on the death of his father a short time ago and would not be of age for another month or two. The Lady Sarah was betrothed and would marry shortly.

"Her father did at least manage that before his death," Richard Moxton had remarked.

"What do you mean?" Stephen had

asked. Richard Moxton was known to be one of the biggest gossips in town.

"The old Earl was not noted for his wisdom in the management of his own affairs or the affairs of anyone else. He was so blatantly Royalist that he lost most of his estate in taxes and fines. That is why his children are now living in a hunting-lodge on the edge of a marsh." Richard had informed him.

"Poor Uncle William!"

"Yes," Richard had eyed him over his tankard. "Two similar situations to sort out! Take my advice and marry a rich heiress instead. You have a title, my lord, albeit an empty one!"

Stephen had ignored the jibe. "The thought had crossed my mind but I need a habitable house before I can take a bride."

"So there is a girl?"

"Probably married by now." The memories of Lucy were faded but pleasant.

"And where might this damsel live?"

"Strangely enough, in King's Lynn!"

"May your mission there be doubly blessed!"

To this they had both raised their tankards.

As he turned in through a pair of sagging gates and rode along the drive Stephen thought longingly of the luscious Jess at the inn the previous night — a memory in no way faded. Jess was a peach of a girl. From the moment her warm brown eyes had met his across the foaming mug she had drawn for him he had felt a thrill of anticipation. Stephen was not as given to tumbling maids in the hay as were some of his fellows but this time he had not hesitated. Nor had he been disappointed. The girl had a body as firm but as soft as a ripe peach — and tanned to the colour of a peach-stone in places where no lady's would have been. Beautiful Jess and a night of bliss. But that was last night — tonight would be very different.

Stephen's arrival was expected. As he turned into the stable-yard a boy ran forward to take his horse and an elderly manservant came to conduct him into the house. Stephen, stiff and tense, followed him in through a side door, along a short passage and into a small parlour.

The sombre-clad group sitting round the fire became silent and a dog growled. Stephen, looking for his uncle, did not at first recognise him. When he did he received a shock.

The William Perrington he remembered had been a tall, well-built man who had towered above Stephen as a boy. Now Stephen, grown to several inches above six feet, looked down on the thin frail man who was so stooped he seemed to have shrunk to half his former size. His hair, once almost as dark as Stephen's black locks, was white.

Mr Perrington came forward to greet his nephew and there was no mistaking the apprehension in his eyes. He had understood the snub of the unanswered letter.

"Welcome, Stephen! You have come a long way to seek us out? But your aunt was delighted by the news of your coming. It has done her a world of good."

"My aunt is ill, sir?" Stephen, his voice stiff with shock, bowed formally. He ignored his uncle's question.

"She had a touch of lung congestion

and we have persuaded her to keep to her room tonight but you may see her as soon as you have supped. Now come and meet Thomas and Sarah, cousins of yours by marriage."

Mr Perrington stepped aside and Stephen found that he was being regarded steadily by two pairs of somewhat wary golden-brown eyes. The Lady Sarah was seated with an enormous grey cat on her lap. The eyes of the animal were almost the same curious topaz colour as hers.

The girl, sitting immobile beneath the cat's weight, had caught the tension between uncle and nephew and wondered at it. The young man was as tall, dark and craggily handsome as the King was said to be; however there the resemblance ended for the visitor was finer-boned and his eyes were a deep sapphire blue. Deeper than . . .

Suddenly aware that Stephen was looking at her, Sarah dropped her own gaze and pushed the cat aside. It stalked over to the hearth and lay down next to a large hound already sprawled there. The animals made a peaceful picture and some of the tension left Stephen.

Sarah rose and curtsied and Stephen, bowing over her hand, said quietly: "My sympathy on the loss of your father, Lady Sarah. I apologise for thrusting myself upon you at a time like this but my business with my uncle is urgent."

"Thank you, my lord. A cousin is always welcome. I trust you did not have too unpleasant a journey?" The polite words were so cool that Stephen wondered fleetingly if she did resent his coming.

There was no mistaking the warmth of the new Earl of Gerton's welcome.

"I'm glad you did brave the ride from London, cousin. There's not many who care to cross the Fens and it will be a pleasure to hear all the latest news!" Stephen smiled. It was obvious that the youth was bored from being boxed up with only his elderly uncle as male company. Seeing him standing next to his sister, Stephen thought they might have been twins. Similar in height and feature, they both had the reddest hair Stephen had ever seen. Their eyes differed, Thomas having the traditional light blue eyes that so often went with red hair. Sarah, the elder by a year of two, had a tiny mole or beauty spot high on her left cheek.

"The latest news is not particularly startling but the ride no doubt did me good, even if the mud did not improve my temper!" Stephen said, still smiling at the eager look on the young man's face.

Sarah went over to the bell-rope and tugged it.

"You must be cold and wet, my lord. Burnet will show you to your room. Your man arrived some hours ago and no doubt will have finished unpacking for you by now. We have had the supper held back and will sup when you are ready."

Stephen bowed. "Thank you. It will be a relief to get rid of this mud. I am afraid I'm no fit object for your ladyship's parlour."

"We are used to mud, my lord. Those who live in a marsh have to be." Again the words were a polite formality.

Washed and changed, Stephen made his way downstairs a little later and found the family waiting for him in the hall. Another man had joined the group. He was dressed in black, as were the others, and Stephen supposed that he must be a close relative. However, when he turned round, Stephen saw he was wearing the garb of a Catholic priest.

Thomas introduced him.

"Lord Ansell, permit me to present Father O'Brien, our mother's cousin, who attempted to tutor us in our younger days. He was forced to leave Ireland during Cromwell's occupation."

Stephen bowed, noting the priest's strong resemblance to his young relatives. The fire of his hair was now dimmed by plentiful streaks of white but in his youth it must have been every bit as red as the young Perrington's. His eyes were tawny and held the same slightly wary expression Stephen had noticed in the Lady Sarah's. Stephen was not surprised that the old Earl had harboured a Catholic priest during the past troubles — Richard Moxton had indicated that the old man had had more heart than sense.

The meal passed pleasantly enough in small talk, to which the Lady Sarah contributed little. When the final dishes had been removed and the wine drunk Thomas took Stephen upstairs to see his aunt.

Mrs Perrington was sitting in a big chair near the fire. She looked smaller and thinner than Stephen remembered her but in contrast to her husband she had aged little. Her thick hair was almost unmarked by grey and her eyes were as bright as ever. She held out her hands to Stephen who moved swiftly to her side and clasped them in his own.

The moment of emotion passed and she looked up at him quizzically.

"My dear, it is good to see you at last and to know that you have come safely through all the troubles. But what brings you all the way to Norfolk?"

"Why, you, Aunt, of course!"

"Come, come, Stephen! You always were an affectionate boy but I don't for one moment believe you came all this way for the love of an old woman!" There was reproach beneath the banter. Clearly she knew about the letter Stephen had ignored.

He stood looking into the fire, wondering how best to make her understand.

She saved him the trouble.

Lying back against the cushions, she said quietly: "You needn't be ashamed of your feelings towards your uncle, Stephen. It must have been a great shock to you to learn that the uncle you respected had joined your father's enemies and deserted his King. But at the time he joined Parliament he honestly believed that some reform was much needed. He did take up arms against his King, it is true, but he had no intention that harm should come to the person of His Majesty. Indeed he had no part in condemning the King."

Stephen took a chair opposite her.

"How did he manage that?" he inquired brusquely. "I had no notion that he had turned his coat."

"He had no choice in the matter. Whether he would have actually 'turned his coat' as you put it and gone to the King's defence I don't know. At Marston Moor he was thrown from his horse and his back was broken. That he can walk again is a miracle that took several years but at the time of the hostilities and of the execution of the King he was far too ill to raise his standard for either cause. Indeed he will never raise his hand against any man ever again. Surely you can see that for yourself?"

Stephen had the grace to look ashamed.

"I was shocked by the change in him," he admitted. "But because he was incapacitated at the time of the King's trial and didn't actually take part in condemning His Majesty does not mean he is any the less guilty."

"You're determined to condemn your uncle, aren't you, Stephen?" his aunt said sadly. "I don't blame you, but let me finish my story before you make final judgement."

"Go on."

"Lying there helpless, your uncle had more than enough time to think and he gradually came to realise what a dangerous monster had been released in giving ultimate power to Parliament. He realised that whoever ruled had to introduce unwelcome laws and taxes and that, born to the job or elected, most men were equally greedy. After a lifetime of training the King was a professional, whereas most of the newly elected Members of Parliament were amateurs — that was the only difference."

"If he came to think in this way why didn't he send assistance to the King? I think I am right in saying he did not do this?"

"He did not. But for this you must blame me, not your uncle."

"You, Aunt Bess? I would have thought you would have been loyal to the King!"

"Sometimes one has to be loyal to one's family — or thinks one has to be," Mrs Perrington said with a sigh. "Rightly or wrongly, for my sake and the children's I begged him to keep silent about his change of mind. It was already too late to help Charles I, and his son was safely away in France. Parliament ruled here with relentless sequestrations and fines for Royalists. I was faced with bringing up a young family and ministering to a helpless husband, so I persuaded him that, unless we were actually asked for help by Cromwell, we would keep quiet about our Royalist sympathies. That is how we come to have our fortune intact, Stephen. If you must condemn your uncle, let it be for his weakness in giving way to my pleading."

Stephen reached out and again took her hand in his.

"I cannot condemn you, Aunt. 'Tis I who should be condemned for not hearing both sides of the story before sitting in judgement."

She saw the shame and compassion in his eyes.

"Why did you come to visit us, Stephen?" she asked gently.

"I came to ask Uncle William to help me set my estate affairs in order. Matters at Deeford are in a sorry state and I've been away too long to know where to begin."

"So you had to put your pride in your pocket?"

He gave her a rueful smile. "Touché! I think we are going to have to follow Charles's policy of 'oblivion' and leave the past to the past."

Mrs Perrington tacitly agreed.

Stephen went on: "I went to London thinking to find you there. Your steward told me where you were visiting, so as needs must and trusting to young Gerton's hospitality I ventured to seek you here. Now I find you unwell, Aunt?"

"Just a touch of old age, plus the marsh ague. Also the physician is a fusspot! I intend to go out tomorrow."

"With care, I hope!"

She ignored him. "So you came home to a worthless inheritance? A poor reward for your father's life and for your years spent in Charles's service!"

Stephen shrugged. "I have my lands intact, which is more than many have, plus a barony and a small grant into the bargain. Charles is fully aware of those who served his or his father's cause but it is quite beyond him to make full restitution to everyone. Some have done better than others admittedly but then some did more than others. My contribution was small and I certainly did not expect a barony for it. That I would have preferred a larger grant is beside the point.

"If he gave less generously to his mistresses he would have more for those who deserved it!" Mrs Perrington said tartly. "Personally I think His Majesty sometimes carries his policy of 'oblivion' too far!"

Stephen had to laugh. "You're a real fire-eater, Aunt Bess!"

"What if I am! It's your interests I'm thinking about!"

"Perhaps Charles would give me letters-of-marque to go privateering. That is something I do know about and 'tis said to be one of the quickest ways of making a fortune!"

"Stephen! You're not serious?" Mrs Perrington sat upright in horror.

"No, my dear, calm yourself. But something will have to be done quickly if I am not to lose a good part of my land. I hope Uncle will be able to show me where to begin. I have done what I can with the King's purse plus what little I had saved, but so much is needed. If I can only get the place producing again I am sure I can carry on from there. Unfortunately stock, seed and repairs take money, vast amounts of it." He rose and began to pace between the bed and his chair.

Mrs Perrington sank back against the

cushions but her eyes never left Stephen's face.

"Stephen, if your uncle offers you money, please take."

"Isn't that what I've come to beg for?"

His aunt caught the bitterness in his voice and made a little placating movement with one hand against the chair arm.

"I know how you must feel about taking something which you think does not rightfully belong to us, but don't you see? Your uncle feels this way too. If you would take the money it would help tremendously to ease the burden of our guilt. It is far too late to help Charles I and His present Majesty doesn't need our help, but you lost your fortune helping your King and if we could help you it would mean a great deal to us both."

Stephen came to an abrupt halt. Put that way it sounded perfectly logical to take money from his uncle but deep inside him he still revolted at the idea. In time his feelings might adjust but at the moment he knew he could not accept an outright gift, no matter how small. However he could not ignore his aunt's pleading. She looked completely exhausted, her face white and drained, only her eyes still expressive.

"I will try and see it your way, Aunt Bess," he assured her gently. "Now I am going to leave you, before I exhaust you into a relapse."

"No, Stephen. I may be tired but you have done wonders, believe you me." She too spoke quietly but he could see that his last words had reassured her. She added, with something like her old sparkle: "Have you considered taking a wealthy bride?"

"I have given it thought!"

"Well, you won't find one in this house!" his aunt informed him.

Stephen smiled. "So I have been told! Don't worry, Aunt, I already know the Lady Sarah is betrothed."

"We are attending a small supper party tomorrow night. Perhaps you will meet someone!"

Perhaps he would meet Lucy again. Aloud he said: "We must see what Lady Luck produces!" He had no wish to pursue the topic, so he bade his aunt good night and let himself out of the room. Below, the hall was deserted and the house very quiet except for a muffled hub-hub from afar off, probably from the servants quarters. The cheerful fire that had been alight before supper was out.

Stephen had no difficulty in finding the small parlour. Only his uncle sat dozing by the fire of his cousins and Father O'Brien there was no sign. Mr Perrington woke with a start as Stephen pulled up a chair and held his hands out to the blaze.

Stephen said without preamble: "Sir, I must ask you to forgive me for not answering your letter. Aunt Bess has fully explained all the circumstances to me and I ask your forgiveness for prejudging you."

The apology was sincere, if rather stiffly worded, and Mr Perrington's lined face relaxed its wary look.

He said quickly, not trying to hide his relief: "It was not prejudgement, nephew, I did turn my back on my King and the sin weighs heavy with me still. Nothing will ever exonerate me from what I did, but if I can serve you in some way it will be both a personal pleasure and a salve to my conscience."

"Shall we agree that the past is past, sir?" Stephen said, acutely embarrassed.

To his relief his uncle took the hint and, settling himself more comfortably into his chair, asked tactfully: "I take it that you need some advice on your estate problems?"

Stephen plunged into a brief outline of his troubles and Mr Perrington heard him out in silence. At the end of the recital his uncle, looking at the lean and tanned profile turned half from him, felt a stab of pity. The Restoration had been a mixed bag of blessings for many. How distressing, in the flush of victory, to have to confess a need of help to your former enemy!

He asked: "Have you any figures here with you, my boy?"

Having braced himself for the offer he was not ready to accept, Stephen rose in quick relief.

"Yes, Uncle. I'll find them for you if I can."

Stephen went quietly across the stone-flagged hall. He had no wish to disturb the profound silence which now engulfed the house. At the top of the stairs he paused. The centre of the gallery was brightly lit by a candelabrum but the light barely reached the arches at each end of the long room. To his right was an archway which doubtlessly led to the family wing. In this archway for a moment the pale oval of a human face seemed to float in the dimness, then it was gone — Stephen blinked, wondering if he had really seen it. A servant, he supposed, as he fetched the necessary papers from his room — When he recrossed the gallery on his way downstairs the archway was empty.

Sometime later the parlour door opened and the young Earl walked in looking rather flustered. "Please forgive me for neglecting you, cousin. There was trouble in the servants' hall. Near came to blows . . . " He walked over to the fireplace and stood staring into the flames.

Mr Perrington looked up. "Domestic trouble or a drainage flare-up?" he asked.

"Oh, drainage. Fanworth has some new scheme the village is up in arms about." Thomas frowned into the flames.

"Well, be thankful you are not beset by drainage problems as they are here, my boy." Mr Perrington remarked to Stephen.

"Yes, from what I've seen, any kind of farming hereabouts must be difficult. But surely if the land is being drained it benefits everyone?"

"No, not always. The land that lies below that which is being drained tends to become more waterlogged. Because the land is so flat and the fall to the sea so slight the rivers flow sluggishly at the best of times. Extra water from higher up makes the rivers overflow their banks lower down. Also it causes them to silt up, making matters worse. The problems are endless."

"How do you mean?"

"Fenlands that have been drained for farming can no longer be hunted and fished in the same way. The Fenmen who have lost their centuries-old way of life resent this. Rivers that are silted up are no use for water-traffic and the townspeople along their banks are equally resentful."

"And in Fanworth's case they are showing their resentment actively?"

"Yes, but not just in his case. Disruption of drainage works has been going on all over the Fens for years. Admittedly here they are particularly well organised by a leader they call the Black Monk. The Commissioners of Sewers do their best to control the sabotage but they are not entirely successful."

"Mm, they seem to be awaiting a new Commissioner in Lynn at the moment." Stephen went on to tell his uncle and cousin of the cold reception he had received in the town square that afternoon.

2

WHEN Stephen came downstairs the next morning he found his cousins, dressed in riding clothes, waiting for him in the hall. They were bending over a note which lay on the hall table. Their two bright heads seemed to send a glow into the darkest corners of the hall.

Thomas looked up. "Good morning, cousin! I trust you slept well?" He waved the note at Stephen. "Before I forget, we are invited to a supper party tonight. It will be a very small quiet party, but you will be very welcome to come too, I know."

"Of course you will be welcome — an extra peer should more than make up for Mrs Gleeson being obliged to ask me!" Sarah said surprisingly.

The name had meaning for Stephen but Sarah's strange outburst interested him more at the moment.

"The lady doesn't like you?"

"She does not consider me fit company for her daughters."

"Sarah, I'm sure you wrong Mrs Gleeson," Thomas said uncomfortably.

"No, I don't! If you looked other than at Mistress Anne you would see Mama Gleeson's eyes positively light up when she sees you, while she does her best not to see me at all!"

Thomas flushed scarlet. "Just because you . . . !" he began furiously but was stopped short by Sarah, her face suddenly white and frozen.

"Thomas! We have a guest! I think he has heard enough of our quarrels."

But Stephen's curiosity was aroused and he could not resist probing: "Why should Mrs Gleeson have misgivings about you? Your mother must have died some time ago, I think, so if you grew up a tomboy it was no fault of yours."

Sarah shot him a look of scorn. The colour had more than returned to her cheeks.

"Oh, no, my lord! Even here in the depths of the country we have our little scandals. I committed the indiscretion of falling in love with the steward's son and Mrs Gleeson is afraid that I might incite her daughters to do the same!"

With her head held high Sarah swept out of the hall and a moment later the passage door banged behind her.

Thomas would have apologised but Stephen said quickly: "The name, I think, was Gleeson. Would that be Mr Edward Gleeson of King's Lynn?"

"Why, yes. Do you know him?"

"Slightly. Meetings in the King's cause were held secretly at his house. I brought messages from France or Holland several times."

"How exciting!" The awe in Thomas's voice betrayed his youth.

Stephen thought of the mad tidal races between the sandbanks of the Wash. In the dark the danger had been multiplied a hundredfold. He knew he owed his survival more to luck than to his seamanship.

"The trips were often wet and uncomfortable," he said truthfully.

"You sailed with Prince Rupert too, didn't you?"

"Yes. And he isn't the monster most

people think him to be."

Thomas replaced the note on the table.

"If Mr Gleeson knows you you will be doubly welcome," he promised, leading the way down the passage and out into the stable-yard where they were joined by Mr Perrington.

Sarah, already mounted, stared in surprise as a groom led out Stephen's own mount, a big light-coloured bay.

"Heavens! What an enormous great brute! Are you sure he is not a farm horse, cousin? And what a strange colour!" She seemed to have forgotten her bad humour.

Stephen had grown used to jeering remarks being made about his horse. The animal suited him.

Smiling, he twitched Land-Lubber's cream mane. "He probably does have some Flemish in him," he admitted. I brought him from the Netherlands with me. He's big and docile which suits me. He may not be of racing stock but he has one excellent habit — he never wanders."

Thomas, mounting his own horse, laughed. "Can you imagine anyone the size of our cousin riding a smaller horse? He would look like an adult trying to ride a child's pony!"

"Well, the horse does suit your height," Sarah conceded.

As your horse suits you, Stephen thought. Sarah was mounted on a magnificent chestnut mare named Star Lady. The girl, red curls escaping from beneath her hat, and the horse were a colour-matched pair.

As they rode out of the gates they almost collided with a rider about to turn in through them. The plain cut of his dark riding suit instantly proclaimed his Puritan outlook. Thomas and Sarah greeted him without enthusiasm and perfunctorily introduced him to Stephen as a neighbour, Sir George Fanworth. Stephen remembered Thomas mentioning the name the previous evening. The man had a hard look about him and Stephen guessed that he would be ungenerous in his dealings. He explained that he had been supervising the erection of a pumping engine, the plans of which he had recently obtained in Holland.

"It is driven by the wind and heaven

knows we have enough of that here!" he said jubilantly. "In Holland they work well pumping water from field drains to main canals and I see no reason why they should not work as well here. I know you are not worried about drainage on your property, Gerton, but the engine might be of some interest to you, if you would care to see it sometime?"

Sir George's self-satisfied manner irritated Stephen and he felt little pleasure when Thomas replied: "No time like the present!"

The lane was too narrow for them to ride more than two abreast and Stephen, wedged in beside his young cousin, watched Sir George confidently position himself next to Sarah and start chatting to her. He received little encouragement, as she answered him with the barest monosylables, but he seemed to take no notice of her attitude and stayed firmly at her side.

They had nearly reached Sir George's imposing gateway when Stephen, looking to his left, saw a jumble of ruins above the hedge. The ground on that side rose steeply for several feet to a small plateau. Whatever building had once occupied the site must have had a view commanding most of the surrounding countryside.

Mr Perrington, bringing up the rear on his docile mount, saw the direction of Stephen's gaze and called: "Those are the ruins of Banks Priory. It was destroyed during the reign of the last Henry along with the other Catholic institutions he ordered to be pulled down. The land subsequently became the property of the Fanworths, who later sold it to the O'Briens." He lowered his voice and added: "This act of their ancestors has greatly vexed the present Fanworths and they have been trying to buy back their lost acres for some years."

"But you still own the ruins?" Stephen asked, turning to Thomas.

"Oh, yes. We, or rather Sarah, still own the Priory — complete with ghost!" Thomas replied with a grin.

"Ghost?"

"Yes, 'tis said to be the Prior, a Frenchman by the name of Brulac. He was killed resisting King Henry's men. The tale goes that a black-cowled figure still walks in the grounds when the moon is up."

"The same that is supposed to lead the dyke-wreckers? How very convenient!"

"I don't imagine anyone seriously thinks that the leader of the saboteurs is a ghost."

"Maybe not, but a handy disguise all the same," Stephen said slowly, thinking of the face he had seen in the gallery the night before. In the dimness a man heavily cowled in black would give just such an impression of a disembodied face.

They did not turn in at the gates. Sir George led them on into a narrow lane and presently they arrived in the marshy field where the windmill stood in one corner, its great canvas-clad vanes turning slowly in the breeze.

They surveyed the little two-storied tower in silence. Through the door they could see two giant cog-wheels turning smoothly, while from the upper floor came the tumble and squeak of two more. At one side of the wooden tower was a huge wheel with scoops attached to it. These lifted the water from the field drain over a dyke and deposited it in a larger drain leading to the river — the process was slow but efficient.

"Very ingenious," pronounced Mr Perrington, voicing the verdict for them all.

"Diabolically clever!" Sarah spoke softly, more to herself than to the others.

But Sir George heard her.

"What do you mean?" he asked sharply, his face darkening.

Sarah had changed colour too. A tiny spot of angry red had appeared on each cheek.

"You know what I mean! That windmill will bring untold misery to the villagers. Once they only feared flooding in winter but since you started to drain your land into the river they have lived in daily danger of having their homes flooded — now the danger will be a reality. This is the end of the summer and the river is up to the top of its banks now. What do you think will happen in winter with that devilish pump of yours adding hundreds of extra gallons of water to the river every hour?"

"You exaggerate, sweetheart! The

villagers will have to raise their dykes, that is all. They have their problems and I have mine and I intend to solve mine the best way I can. How they deal with theirs is no matter to me, nor can I see it is any concern of yours. After all, they are my tenants!"

"Not from choice, afore God! And as they are your tenants you should be making shift to help them!" Thomas spoke quietly but the others sensed that he was as angry as his sister.

Sir George swung round on him wrathfully.

"Are you presuming to say that I have no right to use as I will the river that flows through my land?"

"No, Sir George, I am not presuming to say that but I am saying that you should not jeopardise the lives and comfort of people who live lower down the river. You have every right to use the pump as you are doing but you should carry the project right through and increase the outflow of the river below the village so that flooding will not occur."

With that Thomas seized his sister's

bridle and led her out of the field.

For a moment Sir George remained dumbfounded, then he called mockingly after Sarah: "Till we meet at the party tonight, sweetheart!"

* * *

That evening Stephen was the first dressed and he wandered down into the empty hall. He was followed not long afterwards by Sarah. Watching her descend the stairs, Stephen thought she looked magnificent. She was tall for a woman but she had a natural grace of movement. There was no trace of stooping or gawkiness in her carriage. The unrelieved black brocade gown worn over a black taffeta petticoat made her skin appear startlingly white. Powder blotted out her usual freckles and the effect was a mask of alabaster.

Mrs Perrington came next. "Just like men to be late!" she said, smiling at Stephen.

"We heard that, Aunt!" Thomas and Mr Perrington were descending the stairs together. "Just because you ladies don't take enough care with your toilette, you blame those who do!" Thomas had obviously taken every care with his appearance.

The Gleeson's house on the outskirts of King's Lynn was large and the main rooms were only partly filled. Stephen was formally introduced to Mrs Gleeson and her elder two daughters, Mistress Lucy and Mistress Anne. Three younger girls hovered in the background.

For a moment Mistress Lucy stared at Stephen unbelievingly, then a smile of recognition lit her face.

"Sir Stephen, I beg pardon, Lord Ansell! How nice to see you again!" she said warmly.

"Mistress Lucy!" Stephen raised her hand to his lips, then moved on. This was not the time nor the place for reminiscing about the past.

"You sly dog!" Mr Perrington said jovially. "I don't believe you really came to King's Lynn to see me at all!"

"I came to King's Lynn because you were not in London, Uncle!"

As things had fallen out, he did not regret the extra journey. Lucy still remembered him out of the dozens of cavaliers who must have passed through her father's house during the past troubles. Mr Gleeson, a cripple from birth, had been unable to help his King actively but secretly he had thrown his house open to supporters of the royal cause. Lucy had waited on the men when they arrived for a meeting, then had calmly kept watch on the street from a front window. Lucy was still unmarried too, it seemed.

Pausing in the doorway of a room that had been set up with card tables, Stephen came face to face with his host.

Mr Gleeson bowed. "Lord Ansell, we have met before in less happy times, I believe!"

Stephen took the glass his host offered him. "The King!"

For several minutes they chatted pleasantly, then Mr Gleeson, noticing a young gentleman dressed in the very latest French manner who was eyeing the tables hopefully, introduced him.

"Lord Ansell, may I present the Comte de Verais? He, I think, is also seeking diversion at the tables!"

"Your servant, milord!" The Comte bowed Stephen to a table.

During the next hour or so Stephen took small interest in the party. The Comte was an expert piquet player and Stephen was no amateur. Stephen, who could not afford high stakes, was relieved to find that the Comte did not seem to wish to gamble deeply either. They were well matched and the little pile of coins seesawed back and forth across the table. The pile was in front of Stephen when, to his surprise, the Comte, staring intently over Stephen's shoulder, almost dropped his cards.

"By the Virgin! What a very beautiful girl!" he ejaculated, his dark eyes ablaze with interest.

Stephen twisted round and was in time to see Sarah and his aunt walk across the open double doorway.

"The Lady Sarah Perrington," he said carelessly.

"You know her?"

"My cousin." Stephen turned back to his cards.

The Comte made no move to resume his hand.

"Is it possible that you could arrange an introduction for me, milord?" he asked eagerly, still staring at the now empty doorway.

Stephen looked at him pityingly. "My cousin is already betrothed, sir."

"But not yet married?"

"No."

"All is fair in love and war, is it not!"

It was Stephen's turn to stare. "You are impertinent, sir," he said coldly.

The Comte nodded ruefully. "You are perfectly right, of course! It is just that I have never seen a more beautiful girl," he said regretfully.

"My cousin has a heart of stone, let me tell you!" Stephen said, softening.

De Verais was not to be put off. "You try, I think, to protect your cousin, milord. The fault is mine! Let me make known to you that I am quite respectable — Mr Francis Duffney will vouch for me. He and his parents spent many years of their exile at my father's house. I am here now on a return visit."

Stephen thought rapidly. Sarah's betrothed obviously was not here tonight and she was looking lonely and bored trailing after her aunt. If no love, how about a little war? He did not doubt that Sarah could deal with any attention she did not welcome. Aloud he said: "Well, sir, I will endeavour to make known my cousin to you but, as I have warned you, she is betrothed and will marry before Christmas."

Reluctantly he laid down his cards and pocketed the modest pile of winnings. The Comte followed him eagerly into the main parlour.

Some kind of rowdy game was in progress, seemingly much enjoyed by its flushed and laughing participants. Stephen and de Verais made their way round the edge of the group, passing Sir George Fanworth on the way. Stephen saw no pleasure in renewing his acquaintance with the man, so with a quick nod he walked on.

Sarah, looking up at the young man her cousin introduced to her, was reminded of the local soothsayer's prediction that she would have a man 'tall, dark and handsome' come into her life. This gentleman was almost as tall as her cousin and his face wore a hopeful, boyish smile. Rather to her own surprise and certainly to her aunt's and cousin's astonishment, when the introductions were over she agreed to partner him in the new game that was starting.

"Well, I'll be damned!" thought Stephen.

Those were almost the exact words that Sir George used as he came up to them but his voice and looks expressed more annoyance than surprise. However he found a chair for Mrs Perrington and stayed talking to her until the game ended.

As the Comte returned Sarah to her aunt, supper was announced. As if on cue, Sir George stepped forward and offered Sarah his arm.

"My prerogative, I think, sweetheart!" he said calmly but the words were a command.

For a moment it looked as if Sarah would refuse. Her eyes darkened with anger and she did not move. Then her lashes dropped like a veil and she placed her hand on his arm.

Stephen and de Verais were left

standing looking ruefully at one another. With a shrug the Comte bowed and went off in search of another partner while Stephen offered his arm to his aunt.

"Of all the strange choices! I should have thought the Comte would have been a vastly more entertaining supper partner!" Stephen said explosively.

"But, as Sir George said, it is his prerogative."

"His right? How do you mean?"

Mrs Perrington looked at him in surprise. "Did you not know they are betrothed?"

"Sarah betrothed to Fanworth? No, I did not! And certainly her manner towards him never indicated it!"

Stephen was astounded.

"Maybe not. Nevertheless Gerton bestowed her hand on Sir George before he died."

"Why — to break up her love match with the steward's son? I can understand that the young man was not the most desirable match for an earl's daughter, but Sir George! — she seems to dislike him so. Sarah's father seems to have been a generous man — surely he would not have denied his daughter a love-match?"

Again Mrs Perrington gave him a puzzled look. She opened her mouth to speak, but before she could do so her husband arrived to claim her for supper.

Stephen followed in their wake, his mind in a turmoil. Fanworth of all people! He had formed an instant dislike of the man and he had thought that Sarah shared his dislike. What on earth had persuaded the old Earl to sanction the betrothal? And surely Sarah was legally of an age to marry whom she wished?

At the door of the supper room he found Lucy waiting for him and instantly felt guilty. A party was no place to ponder over news and he had neglected Lucy shamefully.

She smiled at him as she took his arm.

"Lord Ansell, I do hope you found something for your entertainment? I am sure these stupid games are not to your liking at all, but Mama would have them."

"Ah, but she also provided card tables

for the sober-minded, ma'am! I found an excellent opponent in a like-minded Frenchman and my only regret is that I did not notice how the time was passing."

Inside the supper room they met Thomas who was escorting Mistress Anne and in spite of the crush they managed to stay together during the meal. Supper proved to be a very pleasant meal. Not only was the food excellent, but Mistress Lucy showed herself to be the perfect hostess. She was not withdrawn like Sarah, nor did she attempt to flirt with him, but chatted away on a variety of topics and was eager to hear about life at Court. As a gentle warning Stephen touched lightly on his present penniless estate. At the end of the meal Lucy excused herself, saying that she must help her mother get the games going once more.

Stephen, suddenly feeling pent up in the warm crowded room, had a great longing to slip away and smoke a pipe, a habit he had picked up while in the West Indies with Prince Rupert. As his pipe and tobacco were back in his room at Banks House, this was impossible, but on arrival, before entering the house, he had noticed a terrace and decided to find a way out to it.

Walking across the hall, he noticed the three younger sisters giggling in a corner beneath the sweep of the stairs and asked them if they could give him the direction.

"Certainly, sir," the eldest replied. "There is a door from the Long Parlour that leads out onto it."

Seeing Mrs Gleeson approaching, Stephen thanked the girls and beat a hasty retreat before the girls' mama could waylay him. Entering the Long Parlour he found that heavy curtains had been drawn across windows and door alike. The middle curtains had the most movement and these he correctly judged covered the door. Pushing his way through, he found himself out on the terrace and wandered across to lean on the stone balustrade which curled up from the wide steps leading down into the garden.

It was a relief to be out of the warm candle-reeking air of the party rooms.

The night, which had been calm and fine when they had started out for the party, had changed. Great billows of cloud were sweeping across the sky. Below, the gardens were black and silent except for the sighing of the trees in the rising wind.

Suddenly Stephen became aware that in the garden beneath the other end of the terrace a couple were quarrelling. The wind made a meaningless mumble of the words but even so Stephen could hear the anger in them.

In a moment of calm he heard the man say tauntingly: "Think yourself lucky I am willing to take you to wife, sweetheart! Not many gentlemen would after your foolishness!"

The girl's voice was impassioned. "You're no gentleman! Do you think I care about your title? If I . . . " The wind snatched away the rest of the sentence.

Again the man's mocking laugh rang out.

Embarrassed, Stephen turned to leave the terrace but he was too late.

The girl had broken away and came

running up the steps. A shaft of light streamed through the curtains as the wind parted them and the girl ran blindly into it. Stephen stood immobilised — the girl was his cousin, Sarah.

3

AS Sarah came running blindly past him Stephen came back to life. He shot out a hand and grabbed her firmly by the arm, swinging her out of the light and into the shadows.

"Whoa!" he said softly, as if to a horse. "You had better not go straight inside. Everyone would see at once that you had been quarrelling." He could feel her arm still shaking with rage beneath his hand.

"Stephen!" she gasped.

However the sense of his words seeped through her angry turmoil and she walked obediently into the darkness at the end of the terrace. For several minutes there was silence. Stephen played with a ribbon on his coat, feeling acutely uncomfortable. He had no wish to become embroiled in a lovers' tiff. Sarah must think he had been eavesdropping. He almost wished he had not interfered. Somehow he did not think she would welcome his knowledge of the quarrel.

Presently there came the sound of heavy footsteps coming up from the garden. Sarah shrank further into the shadows as Sir George paused at the top of the stairs to look about him. Luckily at that moment the curtains blew wider apart and the extra light must have made the shadows more impenetrable, for, cursing, he strode on into the house.

"The swine!" hissed Sarah in a very unladylike manner.

"I'm sorry," Stephen said, still uncomfortable. "I had no idea anyone was down there. I came outside for some air. The garden seemed quite empty."

"He dragged me round from the front door," Sarah's voice was under control but her shaking hands went to the bodice of her dress.

Stephen felt no surprise at this, only that she could even consider marrying the man.

"Forgive me, cousin, it's no business of mine, I know, but if you dislike the man so much why are you going to marry him? You are of age — no one can compel you to marry him. Why don't you quietly go and marry the steward's son? You could go away to some completely different part of the country where no one knows you and if you hadn't much money there are plenty of gentlefolk in those circumstances after the recent troubled times.

"A neat solution, cousin!"

Stephen felt rather than saw Sarah staring at him in the darkness. When she continued her voice was flat and expressionless. "But there is one insurmountable obstacle. John is dead."

"Dead?"

"Yes. He was found shot one night last spring after the villagers had had a session of wrecking Sir George's dykes. There was quite a riot that night with several shots fired."

Stephen could only say inadequately: "I'm so sorry."

Sarah went on, speaking as if it were a relief to talk: "Have you ever looked at someone's body and felt responsible for their death?"

"If he was shot by the rioters how could you possibly be responsible?"

"John was not one of the wreckers — he didn't believe in violence as means to an end. Whatever he was doing there that night, it was not destructive. I am sure he was only there to try to stop the men, Or . . . "

Stephen waited for her to continue.

"Or he was coming across the fields to visit me. I knelt by his body which was left to lie in our hall all night. I wanted to cry but somehow I couldn't. It was as if every tear had frozen within me."

The moon briefly came out from behind the massing clouds. In its cold light Stephen could see Sarah's face set marble-white. He believed her.

Seeking to divert her, he asked gently: "Didn't your father realise the state of your feelings when he sought to have you betrothed to Fanworth so soon afterwards?"

For a moment Sarah's face softened. "You mustn't think too badly of Father — he really hadn't any choice in the matter." She paused as if to choose her words. "I expect that even before you arrived at Banks House you had heard tales of the decline of our fortune during the war and afterwards?"

"I had heard that the Earl did his best

for the King's cause."

"No doubt you also heard that he'd had to sell the greater part of his main estate — to no purpose." There was bitterness in the girl's voice.

"Many others suffered the same at the time. Now the purpose is achieved."

"For the King, yes. But by the Act of Oblivion we are the losers."

"Yet I thought I heard our uncle say that your brother had regained his Northamptonshire lands?"

"He has, but through no agency of the King." The bitterness was still heavy in Sarah's tone. "When Father had sold the main property the enormity of what he had done suddenly came to him. He had been selling bits and pieces of land for years but this time he had sold his son's patrimony. Oh, he still had the wreckage of Gerton Hall and an acre or two of garden and park around it but there was nothing left to support it. Farms, pasturage and tenants had all gone. Father vowed there and then that nothing would ever make him give up my dowry, which is Banks House. It came into the family with my mother and it was her wish that it should go to me as it is not entailed. How I wish that Father had never made that vow."

"Why?" Stephen felt himself floundering.

Sarah tried to see his face in the gloom but the shadows were too dark.

"It is an unlikely tale, so take it how you will, cousin! When the Northampton estate was sold we had no idea who bought it, as the sale was conducted through agents. Imagine our surprise when our neighbour, Sir George, came to Father and said he had purchased the land. And, what was more, he wanted to do a deal — he would exchange the Gerton estate lands for Banks House and its surrounding few acres. At first Father was very tempted but then he remembered that Banks House was to be my dowry. Tom might in time purchase a new estate for himself but there was no hope of my ever getting another dowry."

"But Fanworth must be mad! Surely the Northampton land would be far more valuable than a few acres of marsh?" Stephen was frankly incredulous.

"In actual market value, yes. But to

Sir George Banks House is priceless. It stands in the way of a dream!"

"I've heard talk of marsh-madness — now I believe in it!"

Sarah sighed. "I'm well aware it sounds like madness but actually the reason is quite logical. Banks House is not built on marshland. It's built on a crescent-shaped rocky outcrop or island — you must have heard of the Fen islands like the Isle of Ely? Our particular outcrop lies between Fanworth's land and the sea marsh. But if he could somehow drain through our outcrop or down the side of it directly into the lower part of the river he could reclaim a large tract of land which is now no better than a fen. Sir George has grandiose dreams of becoming another Earl of Bedford or Company of Fen Adventurers in a smaller way."

Stephen perceived the drift of the story.

"And, as you were the owner of Banks House virtually, Sir George decided to have you?"

"Exactly! Only I wasn't having him! I was in love with John and Father knew this. He didn't like the match and would not agree to our betrothal but he refused to force me to marry Sir George — none of us had ever liked the man. We think he spied on us during the Commonwealth, which was why Father was always getting fined. Then John died. Sir George was too clever to rush matters. He left me alone until he realised that Father too was dying. Then he went to him and made a proposition."

A burst of merriment from the room behind them made Sarah stop. She glanced angrily at the open windows and then stood staring out into the darkness.

"The proposition was that you marry him and he would restore the estate lands to your brother?" prompted Stephen when she showed no sign of resuming.

"An inspired guess, cousin! At first Father just laughed at him but, the more Father thought about it, the less he wanted to laugh. It was such a perfect answer to all our troubles. Tom would get his lands back and I would be safely married to a respectable husband, an event which, as Sir George kindly pointed out, would not be so likely to happen, as the whole countryside seemed to know about my falling in love with the son of a steward. It was the thought of leaving me secure and settled that finally won Father over. He begged me to agree — he was dying, so how could I refuse? Besides, at the time I was too numb to care what became of me now that John was dead and Father about to die."

"And now the numbness has worn off?"

"I know now better and better what sort of man I am betrothed to."

"Cannot the agreement be broken? You are of age and can surely refuse to marry him?"

"If I do not marry him Tom will lose his inheritance. Besides, would you have me break the promise I made before my father on his death-bed?"

"Surely it is not so binding that it must ruin your life?"

"My life is already ruined. I may be a female, my lord, but at least grant me my honour!"

"Nay, cousin, don't quarrel with me!" Stephen said hastily, sensing that her temper was rising again. "I'm well aware it's nothing to do with me. I just don't like seeing people unhappy, that's all."

"You're a strange man, cousin! You had better get you hence before you get embroiled in our affairs."

"I intend to leave tomorrow, ma' am," Stephen said stiffly. "My business with my uncle is concluded. I realise that I had no right to take advantage of your hospitality — or to intrude upon your private affairs."

"That is nonsense! You had little choice in either!"

Stephen bowed. "Then perhaps you will explain one more thing to me?"

"What do you want to know?"

"How is it that Gerton already has his lands back when you are not yet married to Fanworth and how is it that your brother is allowing you to sacrifice yourself?"

Sarah stiffened but answered calmly: "I could say it is none of your business, cousin, but I'll tell you in case you start asking questions elsewhere! Please believe me when I say Tom knows nothing of this, nor does anyone else apart from Sir

George. Nor must anyone ever know, least of all Tom. Promise me this?"

"I promise." Stephen had the feeling that he was being rash.

"It was part of the agreement that Tom should get his lands back straight away so that he should never guess what really happened. He thinks Sir George sold the land back to Father for a very low sum — perhaps out of the goodness of his heart for a dying man or, more likely, to ingratiate himself with me. Sir George still holds one vital receipt, which Tom and Uncle think he is having legalised, as he knows about such things, having been a land clerk to Cromwell. Sir George will give the paper to me the night before our wedding so that I can casually hand it over to Tom as if it were a transaction Sir George wanted cleared up before the wedding. We are to be wed early in November, on the day Tom becomes of age."

"Fanworth will trust you not to run away in the night?"

"Perhaps he thinks I cannot get far in one night! No, I have sworn by all that is holy that I will neither run nor wed another man during that night. Now perhaps you can understand why I cannot wittingly break the contract."

"Wittingly?"

But Sarah shivered suddenly. "It's turned cold. Let us go back inside now, please."

Realising that he would get nothing more out of Sarah, Stephen held aside the curtains and they slipped back into the Long Parlour. When they rejoined Mrs Perrington she looked at her niece sharply. Sarah looked tired. Her face was quite colourless and there were dark smudges beneath her lustreless eyes. What had the girl been doing? She had entered the room with Stephen but Mrs Perrington did not think that he was the cause. More likely the girl had had a tiff with her betrothed.

Mrs Perrington beckoned to her other nephew when he wandered past a few moments later. "Gerton, I think we are all getting tired. Will you send for the coach, please?"

"Certainly, Aunt." There was a lack of enthusiasm as he went to do her bidding.

Stephen slipped away to find Lucy. He discovered her and her younger sisters in the supper room supervising the final removal of the food. As soon as she saw him in the doorway she came out to him and for a moment they were alone in a quiet corner of the hall.

"I have seen little of you all evening," he said, trying to make it sound like an apology and not an accusation. "A party is not the place for a reunion. I leave Banks House tomorrow, but may I call on you on my way through King's Lynn?"

"Of course, my lord. You will be very welcome at any time."

"Not in the middle of the night as of old, I trust!"

She laughed. "Those times are over forever, I hope."

"Till tomorrow then." He bowed and returned to his relations.

Of Sir George there was mercifully no sign but the Comte gallantly escorted them to their coach when they had made their farewells to their host and hostess. As they went out through the front door a cold spatter of rain met them, and no one was sorry when the coachman banged the door shut.

There was little said on the way home. Mr Perrington immediately dozed off and his snores were sufficient to inhibit speech if anyone felt like it; those awake had thoughts enough to occupy them.

Sarah, as she sank into a corner of the coach, was aware of several conflicting emotions. She had been foolish to let fly at Sir George and an even bigger fool, she felt, to confide in Stephen. How had it happened? Thank goodness he was leaving tomorrow, or she would have been likely to bitterly regret her stupidity, she was certain.

Deliberately she changed the path of her thoughts to think of Emile de Verais. Long ago old Mistress Fuller had foretold that a man — tall, dark and good to look on — would enter her life. There would be doubt and danger but eventually she would find peace and happiness with him. Sarah had laughed at this. She was in love with John Carr, blond and no taller than her. There would be no other love.

John had died and now she was

betrothed to Sir George, another fair man of average height. But tonight she had met the tall, good-looking man. In the darkness of the coach she seemed to see his eyes caressing her tenderly; no man had looked at her like that except John. Though her thoughts of the Comte warmed her she knew that he had come too late.

Seated opposite her, Stephen was worried. The story Sarah had told him was, as she said, a strange tale but what perturbed him was the certainty that Sarah had left something out. None of the reasons she had given him for marrying Sir George rang completely true. And then there was the question of her dislike of the man and his methods. Would she really just hand him the means of making the largest ever floods and more misery for the local people?

Like Sarah, he forcibly changed the direction of his thoughts. Lucy. During the past year she had matured into a very charming young lady but had her growth been equal to his? Compared to Jess she was still a mere child, though that was of no matter. Somehow, during the short time of his visit on the morrow, he must gage his feelings — and hers — and make a decision. Her dowry was tempting. Mr Gleeson was thought to be a still wealthy man and, as the eldest daughter in a family without sons, her inheritance would be considerable. But there must be more than that.

With a sigh Stephen stretched out his long legs. Sarah had been right when she had told him not to get involved in their troubles — he had enough of his own. One he had settled that day. He had agreed to accept an interest free loan from his uncle — a solution which had satisfied them both. His pride was almost intact; his uncle's burden of guilt was lightened.

Before they reached Banks House the rain came teeming down, backed now by a strong wind blowing in from the North Sea. They all got drenched and chilled on their quick dash from the coach to the front door, which had been flung wide by a sleepy Burnet.

Sarah, seeing her aunt shiver, called for fresh warming-pans for the beds and for the bedroom fires to be banked up.

She hastily shepherded Mrs Perrington upstairs where she left her in the capable hands of her serving-woman, while she returned downstairs to the kitchen to brew her aunt a hot posset. The gentlemen were served with mulled wine.

It was almost dawn before the household slept.

4

SARAH, exhausted chiefly by her outburst of temper, slept deeply though not for long. She was awakened by a frantic message from Mr Perrington informing her that her aunt had taken ill again. Sarah pulled on her clothes to the sound of rain and of wind shrieking round the house — a sound which did nothing to ease her mood of depression.

Depression gripped the whole household during the following days. The physician came out from King's Lynn but he had no reassurances for them — Mrs Perrington was very ill and remained so for more than a week. Her serving-woman and Sarah nursed her day and night while Tab, Sarah's maid, acted as housekeeper. Stephen put off his departure for Deeford and, suspended in a vacuum of anxiety, the men fiddled about from room to room, unable to settle to a game of cards or chess. Belatedly Stephen remembered to send a message to Lucy to explain why he had not visited her.

Suddenly one evening Sarah appeared in the parlour doorway.

"Uncle! Aunt is better! The fever broke about an hour ago and now she is asleep. She has even taken a few mouthfuls of broth! Dr Somers says that if she does not have a relapse during the next few days there is every hope."

"Heaven be praised!" said Father O'Brien thankfully and dropped to his knees on the parlour floor. The others willingly followed suit, unmindful of their own religious denominations.

The following evening Sarah ate in the dining-parlour for the first time in more than a week. Still feeling weary, she seated herself in the chair Burnet held for her as the men gathered round the table. Mr Perrington and Father O'Brien were pleased to see her, she thought, but her brother and cousin seemed so sunk in their own thoughts that they hardly noticed she was there.

Sarah waited a while, then asked: "What's the matter, Tom?"

Thomas laid down his knife. "We

rode to the village this afternoon and found the whole place under water. It had got into most of the houses and even into the church. The depth of the water isn't dangerous but it is damaging property, besides making conditions very uncomfortable."

He ate a mouthful, then continued: "The water just keeps swilling over that bit of low bank near the bridge. The men reckon the level of the river is steadily rising. They have been to Fanworth to beg him to stop the windmill, if only for a few hours, but he refused. Stephen and I decided to see if we could make him change his mind . . . "

He choked and Stephen took up the tale. "We found him superintending some minor repairs to the pump and when he saw us he didn't look very welcoming. Thomas came straight to the point and asked him to shut the thing off for a while. You would have thought Sir George was going to take a fit! He bellowed that no one was going to stop the pump while his land was under water and that if we were so concerned with the villagers' conditions we could go and fill sandbags to stop the flow!"

"You'll never move Sir George with words," Sarah said with conviction.

She spoke without much heat but Thomas looked worried.

"Oh, come, Sarah! I know I was enraged by his stubbornness and lack of sympathy but there must be some way to make him see reason."

"Or some way to help the villagers," Sarah said thoughtfully.

Thomas eyed his sister anxiously. "Of course something will have to be done," he said soothingly. "But let's leave it until tomorrow, shall we? It has stopped raining and the level of the water may fall during the night."

Stephen had the impression that he was hearing a veiled warning. Whether or not it had any effect he did not know, for Sarah changed the subject to talk about their aunt's progress, then sat back and said little more during the meal.

When Thomas and Stephen returned to the village the next morning to see what could be done to raise the river banks they found their help was not needed. The river had dropped below its banks during the night and the village was no longer under water. There was mud and slush everywhere but apart from a few women who were trying to sweep the mud from their cottages no one was making much effort to clear up. A sullen silence hung over the place, broken only by the angry mutterings of a group of men gathered in front of the church.

Thomas walked his horse over to them. "What ails you, men? Aren't you pleased the river has stopped flooding?"

"Ay, we're pleased, my lord, but . . . "

A middle-aged man rode up from the opposite direction. He was considerably better dressed than the rest of the villagers and Stephen guessed he must be the Perringtons steward, James Carr.

"Good-morning, my lords. I fear our troubles are not yet over. There was an attack on Sir George Fanworth's pumping engine last night. The sails were cut from the windmill and a dyke was broken down, letting the river water flood back into his fields. He is so angry that he has sent another report to the Commissioners of Sewers and he has threatened to have those responsible for the damage flogged."

Thomas looked worried. "He hasn't caught the culprits?"

"No, my lord, but he means to find out who they are."

"He will have no easy task. I imagine no one here will inform."

"I think not, my lord. Everyone in the village swears they were within doors last night and even Mr Jeffreys, the parson, says he heard nothing. But if Sir George does not find the men who did the damage there are plenty of other ways he can take his revenge on the village people. He is their landlord."

"Unfortunately true! However, first things first. I should worry about raising the river banks before the flooding starts again. Sir George suggested that a few sandbags might be useful!"

Stephen grinned at his cousin's watered down version of Sir George's remark but he knew Thomas was worried. He was still frowning when they arrived back at Banks House.

Dinner was a far more cheerful meal than they had had for many days. Sarah was able to report that Mrs Perrington was progressing satisfactorily — news which caused a general rise in spirits. Thomas alone seemed preoccupied and Stephen was hardly surprised when he steered his sister apart after the meal and vanished into the library with her, no doubt to beg her to intercede on behalf of the villagers with her betrothed. Not that she would get far, Stephen thought angrily. As the days passed he liked Sir George less and less.

Passing the library door on his way to the stables a short time later, Stephen thought he heard Sarah's voice raised wrathfully but when she and Thomas came running out to join him a few minutes afterwards both looked pleased with themselves and in complete harmony.

On returning to the house they found the Comte de Verais had just arrived. He had come, he said, to enquire after the health of Mrs Perrington, having heard that she had taken ill, but Stephen, seeing him linger over Sarah's hand, was inclined to believe that he had come more to visit her than to enquire about their aunt.

"I would have been here yesterday," de Verais apologised. "But I got myself lost in coming. Francis is away for a few days and Sir Peter was unable to accompany me. He gave me very careful directions how to find the road across the marsh and this road I found all right, but then I must have turned up the wrong lane. When I came to a large house and knocked to find out where I was I found the house belonged to Sir George Fanworth. Naturally I asked to pay my respects to him and first he insisted I see his pumping engine and after that I must drink wine with him. By then it was too late to visit you, so I have come today instead."

"What did you think of his windmill?" enquired Sarah, calmly withdrawing her hand which the Comte had held during his lengthy explanation.

"I thought it was an instrument of the Devil!" said de Verais frankly. "It is not natural to move water in such a manner. It leaves his fields dry, yes, but somewhere else would be made very wet."

"Exactly! We also told him it is a machine of the Devil," Sarah said with a little smile.

"And should be sent right back to the Devil!" There was an angry gleam in Thomas's eyes.

Sarah shook her head at him imperceptibly and the talk turned to an invitation to the Comte to sup with them in two night's time. Later than that and Stephen would be gone, he told them. Their aunt was making good progress and already he had stayed away from Deeford too long.

During the remainder of the afternoon and the early evening Stephen had the feeling that Thomas and Sarah were planning something. Thomas was evasively busy and Sarah more animated than usual, though this could be due to the Comte's visit.

After supper the family divided up much as usual. Sarah went upstairs to her aunt while Father O'Brien accompanied Stephen and his uncle to the fireside of the small parlour, as Thomas wanted the library to finish some work on estate papers which the Comte had earlier interrupted.

"Let them wait until the morning, my boy. We can make short shift of them then," Mr Perrington suggested.

Thomas shook his head. "I must get used to managing for myself, Uncle. If I get too badly stuck perhaps you would help me tomorrow?"

Mr Perrington allowed the matter to drop at that. However about halfway through the evening he decided that they needed Thomas to take a fourth hand at cards. Father O'Brien rose and went to the library to fetch him.

Father O'Brien was soon back — and in a state of high indignation. "The young puppy!" he snorted disgustedly. "Come and see what you think of him!"

Mystified, Stephen and Mr Perrington made their way to the library. Mr Perrington came to a standstill just inside the threshold and Stephen was forced to peer over his uncle's shoulder.

The room was hot and smelt strongly of wine and candles. Two bunches of these burned on the mantelshelf behind the massive oak writing-table and a third candelabrum stood on the table itself, lighting the chaos. A mass of papers had been pushed untidily to the back of the table. Taking their place in the cleared area was one obviously empty wine bottle, one still containing wine and an overturned goblet with a runnel of wine reaching almost to the edge of the table. In the chair behind this mess sat Thomas. His head lolled backwards and sideways, supported by the high chair-back and his left hand. He was snoring gently and was undoubtedly very sound asleep. On top of the bookshelf crouched the big grey cat, its tail flicking with displeasure at the invasion.

Mr Perrington broke the verbal silence. "Disgusting! The young devil! Who would have thought it?"

He stepped round the table and shook Thomas, who only grunted and flopped lower into the chair, his supporting hand slipping from beneath his head, which was left at an uncomfortable-looking angle.

Stephen sauntered over and pushed the dangling hand back up against his cousin's face. "He will get a crick in the neck if he is left like that," he observed seriously.

But it was all he could do to keep from laughing aloud. More suspicious of the scene than the others, he had noticed, in spite of a coating of some cosmetic, the give-away mole on his cousin's cheek. Luckily that side of his cousin's face was in shadow — and Mr Perrington was too busy giving vent to his indignation.

He rounded on Father O'Brien who had followed them into the room. "Dead drunk! I should have thought you would have kept a better eye on the boy and kept him from habits like this!"

"Ah, but he is a boy no longer! Nor have I ever known him to drink this deeply before." Father O'Brien frowned down at the unconscious figure before leading the way out of the room.

Stephen glanced back into the library before he closed the door. His cousin had not moved but was making sounds of choking rather than snoring.

Mr Perrington and the priest returned to the parlour, Father O'Brien with the intention of summoning Burnet to get the Earl taken up to bed.

Stephen did not re-enter the parlour with them but slipped back along the passage and silently opened the library door. The mess on the desk had not been touched but the Earl was no longer seated in his chair. He had pulled aside one of the heavy curtains and was about to climb out of the window, but hearing the sound of the door opening he stiffened.

"So!" Stephen said, advancing into the room. "You're not as drunk as you made out to be — my lady cousin!"

"You did guess, cousin — I thought you did," Sarah said coolly, her amber eyes regarding him with amusement. "No, I'm not in the least drunk. I only had one mouthful and then spilled some down my shirt for the right effect!"

"You certainly succeeded in disgusting everybody!" Stephen said, not disguising that this was his sentiment. "I suppose that at this moment Thomas is dressed in a black robe and is wrecking Sir George's windmill. The other day I got the feeling that the villagers were led by someone from Banks House. The first night I arrived I saw a cowled figure vanish into the family wing. If I remember correctly Thomas was not with us that evening until late."

Sarah's look of amusement changed to one of anger.

"I don't care what you saw that night! It wasn't Tom, nor is he wrecking the windmill tonight. He doesn't believe in violence any more than John did. Tom won't have anything to do with the raids, he never has."

"Then why this masquerade?"

"Just a joke. We used to dress up in one another's clothes sometimes to fool Father O'Brien and Papa. Tom wanted to go out tonight with no questions asked and we thought this would give him an alibi if anyone came looking for him. It's not easy being constantly watched by two elderly guardians."

Stephen could see the truth in this — at Thomas's age he had been a free agent. All the same, it was too neat. If he was not actually wrecking the windmill Thomas could be involved in some other mischief.

"Well, I hope you're right — that Gerton isn't meddling in something which could land him in serious trouble.

I don't know what the authority of the Commissioners of Sewers is but I assume they must have some punitive powers?"

"I very much doubt if Sir George would actually call in the Commissioners — they would probably force him to spend money to improve the village flood conditions! But I promise you, Tom is not leading a sabotage raid."

"Nevertheless it will mean trouble if he is caught doing anything unlawful tonight."

"But he won't be."

Sarah sounded positive, so Stephen decided to leave it and try a new attack. "The results would not have been very pleasant if you had been caught out either. Making a fool of your uncle is hardly polite hospitality!"

Sarah flushed. "Stop moralising, cousin! It's none of your business!"

"Well, I'm making it my business enough to tell you it is more than time you disappeared from this room!"

At that moment the cat sat up, his ears pricked. In one swift movement he jumped down from the bookshelf, rubbed himself briefly against Sarah's legs, then went and stood by the curtains waiting to be let out. As Sarah lifted the curtain she and Stephen heard a footfall at the far end of the passage.

"Burnet knows," Sarah said and followed the cat out into the night.

There was no movement in the curtains when the door opened and Burnet came in, a cloth over his arm. He betrayed no surprise at finding Stephen alone in the room.

"Your . . . er . . . master has retired, Burnet!" Stephen felt slightly foolish.

"Very good, my lord." Burnet went over to the table and began to mop up the spilt wine.

Stephen left him to his task and returned to the small parlour. He found to his relief that his uncle and the priest were on the point of retiring to bed.

"Have you managed to get the young rascal to bed?" asked Mr Perrington.

"He is being taken care of. No doubt he will repent of his night's work in the morning!" Stephen replied with more truth than he knew.

He did not care for the keen look Father O'Brien gave him but the priest asked no questions, merely bowing good-night as he left the room. Probably he guesses, Stephen thought.

Stephen and his uncle collected their bedroom candles from the hall table and made their way upstairs together. Stephen glanced along the gallery towards the other wing as they reached the top of the stairs; however the darkness in the far arch was unbroken. He bade his uncle good-night and went into his own room.

Once Stephen was attired in his nightshirt he dismissed Morris but did not get into bed immediately. Instead he crossed over to the window and drew back the curtains. Outside the night was very dark, with only a slight breeze. There had been a fairly new moon that evening — he remembered seeing it before he had come indoors. It had long since set but even while it was up it would have given little or no light. Certainly not enough to have hindered any sabotage of the windmill.

Had the affair just been a stupid joke? Again Stephen guessed that Sarah had not told him everything. She had vowed that Thomas was not mixed up with the saboteurs, yet both brother and sister openly sympathised with them. The young fools, meddling in criminal activities, even if they did agree with the cause. Probably they both knew who the Black Monk was.

Stephen jerked the curtains back into place. As Sarah had pointed out, it was not his affair. He would be gone within the next few days.

5

THOMAS was not seen the next morning until the rest of the family were ready mounted. Stephen, his mind still running on Sir George's vengance, was about to ask Sarah where he was when he came drifting into the stable-yard looking suitably pale and bleary-eyed. Stephen mentally gave him full marks for his appearance.

"Oh, there you are, you young dog!" Mr Perrington said testily. "We'd begun to think you couldn't stand a little wine. Not feeling so good this morning, eh? Teach you a good lesson!"

"How right you are, sir!" Thomas swung himself slowly up into his saddle, assisted by his groom, and closed his eyes artistically as he did so.

The cavalcade rode out into the lane. It was a sunny morning and in spite of the keen wind they decided to head for the marsh. They had nearly reached the turn-off when there came the sound of a horse being ridden full tilt towards them. A moment later Sir George came galloping round a bend in the lane. When he saw them he drew rein so sharply that his horse slithered to a halt only a couple of yards from Stephen.

Stephen was shocked at Sir George's appearance. The man's usually florid face was a pale sickly yellow and his forehead glistened with a fine film of sweat. He looked as if he had been frightened half to death. When he spoke there was a tremble in his voice, caused by fear or rage.

"They've gone too far this time!" he gasped as he drew breath.

Stephen had an unpleasant prickle of foreboding but Thomas asked calmly: "Who have gone too far and doing what?"

Sir George looked at him with a mixture of suspicion and suppressed rage.

"Come and see for yourselves what has been done. Yes, you come too, sweetheart!" he added roughly to Sarah, who would have left the group. "The sight of your friends' handiwork may sicken you towards them somewhat!"

Sarah glanced at her brother but he only shrugged and turned his horse to follow Sir George.

Without another word he led them along the lane and through the fields to a space near the windmill. Here a couple of men came forward to take their horses. Sir George lifted Sarah down, a sneering look coming into his eyes when she stiffened at his touch.

"You haven't long left to put on your airs and graces, my lady!" he whispered in her ear as he set her on her feet.

Sarah knew what he meant. Without replying she lifted her skirts up out of the mud and started to walk towards the windmill.

Thomas tried to catch her up but Sir George grabbed him by the arm. "Not so fast! It's almost as if you don't want her to see. Perhaps you already know what went on last night!"

Thomas pulled himself free. "If it frightened you, Sir George, it can be no sight for a lady!" he said pointedly.

He was right. Sarah, still ahead of the others, rounded the corner of the windmill and came to a halt with a little gasp, her hands flying to her mouth as if to stop the sound. Thomas leapt forward to her side and as Sir George stepped back the others were left with a clear view.

Nailed to the door of the tower was a large black cockerel. Its throat had been hideously cut and the blood, now dried to a sticky brown streak, had run down the door and over a wooden step to form a dark stain on the ground.

"May the merciful Saints of Heaven preserve us!" gasped Father O'Brien, hastily crossing himself. "'Tis a sign of the Devil himself!"

"Exactly!" said Sir George shortly.

Stephen, catching his breath in a hiss of disgust, had a desire to follow the priest's example. Among superstitious seamen he had heard plenty about black magic and witchcraft but he had never come in actual contact with the evil before. The sight both disgusted and alarmed him. He did not know if he fully believed in the evil eye but that someone had hated Sir George enough to do this to him was an evil in itself. At the back of his mind was the worry that his cousins might somehow be mixed up in it all. Thomas had secretly gone out by himself the night before, leaving Sarah to cover up for him. She was positive he had not been harming the windmill but he could have been seeing to the cock.

Thomas meanwhile, standing with his arm round his sister, said calmly: "I do not know too much about witchcraft but I gather that the forces of darkness have marked your machine as their own, Sir George. The cock, I have heard said, is the creature most hated by sorcerers and the Devil alike."

"Why?" asked Stephen curiously.

"Because its crowing marks the end of the sabbat and calls Christians to their worship."

"You are very knowledgeable!" Sir George, now nearer his normal colour, eyed Thomas closely.

"One hears and reads things," Thomas replied airily.

Sir George glanced at the revolting object which was attracting a steady stream of flies.

"The evil eye nothing!" he burst out. "That is someone's idea to frighten me into stopping the pump. Well, the joke's misfired! There is now one witch less in the village and no amount of dead objects is going to make me stop the windmill."

"I hope you are right and that no dreadful mishap will befall you." Thomas sounded serious enough.

"What do you mean by 'one witch less'?" Sarah broke her silence.

"Signs of witchcraft need a witch to procure them; witchcraft is an offence punishable by the water trial. My men will have, even now, conducted such a trial in the village. The outcome, I trust, will be one old crone less and the villagers will have had a fair example of what I will mete out if anyone dares to touch my pump again!" Sir George's words held a warning and his eyes watched the Perringtons closely.

Neither brother nor sister moved. Both stared at him as if mesmerized. There was a long minute of silence, broken only by the creaking of the windmill, then Sarah asked: "How did you find out who was responsible?"

"I didn't have to. I've heard tales oft

enough that the old woman is a witch. She'll get a fair trial and if she can't prove her innocence I'll be rid of a worthless tenant! The old crone and her brother haven't paid a proper rent in years."

Thomas would have spoken but Sarah dug her fingers into his arm and said tensely: "I think I have heard enough. Will you take me home, please, Thomas?"

Sir George bowed mockingly. "You will have to learn not to be soft-hearted with our rebel tenants, sweetheart!"

Sarah turned on her heel and walked swiftly back to her horse. Nothing was said during the ride back along the lane but when they reached the gates of Banks House Sarah turned to her uncle and Father O'Brien and asked them to excuse her and Thomas as they needed a gallop to blow away the taint of evil.

The two elderly men readily agreed, saying that a glass of wine would revive them best. Stephen was not sure that his cousins wanted his company but, not wishing them to plan more trouble, he followed them on down the lane.

Thomas frowned when he saw Stephen

come up behind him but Sarah said briefly: "Stephen knows about last night, Tom. He saw through my masquerade but he helped me maintain it in front of the others." She kicked her horse into a gallop and the three of them went pounding along the lane to the village.

Drawing rein to cross the bridge they could see that the village was deserted and the river, as far as the eye could see, equally so.

"They're not holding the trial here. Damn!" Thomas said tersely, then shouted at an old man who peered at them from a doorway: "Where have Sir George's men gone to hold the water trial?"

The old man shuffled out to them and, grabbing Thomas's stirrup, babbled something incoherent about his sister.

Thomas reached down and touched the old man's shoulder. "Hush! Tell us where they have gone, man, or we will never be able to save your sister."

"Of course! It must be old Mistress Fuller they have taken. The old lady tells fortunes and tends the sick but she wouldn't hurt an ant, let alone kill a cock like that!" Sarah said savagely.

The old man looked at her gratefully. "'Tis true, my lady. They've taken her to Donnans Pool. She be no witch, but she bain't able to swim neither."

Thomas led the way, his sister and Stephen following. Their path was slightly above the sea marsh, through clumps of bushes and wind-twisted trees. Suddenly there came the sound of shouting and a splash, then a queer silence. Coming out of a group of trees they found the ground took a sudden slight slope. Below, on the edge of the marsh, was a large stagnant pool, its surface almost covered by a greenish scum except where something had been thrown into the water. Here the scum was being churned about as an object sank and rose again to the surface.

On the bank were two groups of people. One, consisting of a crowd of villagers, stood silently watching, as if shocked into immobility; the other, half a dozen or so of Sir George's house servants, shouted taunts as they turned to leave. Their work was done. The widening rings were spreading to the edges of the pool but no new ripple was forming.

Thomas jumped from his horse and went scrambling down the bank, flinging off his cloak and hat as he did so. By the time Stephen and Sarah had followed him down he was already thigh deep in the slimy water. None of the villagers moved to follow him. Although they knew the charge was false no one dared to interfere with a trial for witchcraft. Thomas was soon waist-deep and had to swim a few strokes before he was able to clutch at the now motionless bundle which was floating just beneath the surface. Swiftly he towed it back to where he could stand, then picked it up in his arms and made for the edge of the pool. The deep mud at the bottom of the pool sucked at the added weight and he stumbled several times.

Stephen had waded a few yards out from the edge and together they got the almost unrecognisable body of the old woman onto firm ground. Her hands had been bound tightly behind her back and her feet had been tied to them, right foot to left hand and left foot to right hand. No one in that condition would have had a hope of getting out of the water alive, no matter how well he or she could swim.

Coughing up a mouthful of the foul water he had swallowed, Thomas cut the cords which bound the helpless body with his sword. He paused, not knowing what to do next. The old woman lay without movement, apparently dead. Stephen knelt beside her; he had attended drowning men before. He looked with pity at the shrivelled walnut of a face and at the shrunken body that was scarcely larger than that of a monkey. Her eye-sockets and mouth were full of slime and he rolled her over to clear them, then he slowly began to press her shoulders up and down. Around them there was utter silence. The villagers kept their distance as they watched. Suddenly the old woman coughed feebly and a startled hiss went up from the villagers.

Sarah dropped to her knees on the other side from Stephen, fumbling with the clasp of her cloak as she did so.

"She's still alive, God be praised! We must get her to somewhere warm as soon as possible. Help me wrap her in this."

Together they wrapped the wet form

in the cloak. The old woman whimpered once or twice but her eyes remained closed.

"Here, have mine too," Thomas had picked up his hat and cloak from where he had flung them. He held out his short cloak.

Sarah, seeing him shiver, shook her head. "Best put it on yourself, Tom. You had better ride with her as your clothes are already ruined, so the cloak will do you both. We'll have to take her home. In their present mood none of the villagers will be any use in looking after her and her brother can't manage alone. I'll ride ahead and get things ready."

Thomas mounted and Stephen handed the old woman up to him; even in her wet garments she weighed very little. Stephen lifted Sarah into her saddle and watched her start on her way before he mounted himself. The villagers watched them go, still in silence.

When Thomas and Stephen arrived in the stable-yard quite a little reception awaited them but no one came forward to take the old woman from the Earl while he dismounted. The circle of faces in the yard was as sullen as the villagers had been at the poolside. After a swift glance round Stephen slid from his saddle and took the limp bundle from Thomas. Together they carried the old woman into an empty room behind the stable building and deposited her on some rough coverings that had been laid over a pile of straw.

Sarah, changed into a plain stuff gown, and trailed by her reluctant maid, Tab, followed them into the room.

Casting a quick look at her brother, Sarah said briefly: "Best go and have a hot tub yourself, Tom. I can manage here. Tab will help me."

The last few words were an order and Tab nodded unwillingly but she kept as far away from the old woman as she possibly could. Witches, even suspect ones, were not to be trifled with. Why this one had not been left to drown she could not imagine. She had heard plenty from the other maids about Mistress Fuller and her uncanny prophecies. Goodness only knows what evils the old witch would bring upon the household. The old woman looked harmless enough lying there unconscious but she might even now be communicating with the Devil. Surreptitiously Tab crossed herself before she moved closer to help her mistress.

Thomas was not a pretty sight as he oozed mud and slime across the cobble stones. He looked cold and miserable and somehow very young. Stephen felt sorry for him but he hoped the young fool had learned his lesson. Stephen had not the slightest doubt now that it had been Thomas who had nailed the dead cockerel to the windmill door last night. There was still time for the prank to end in disaster, he well knew. With a slight shiver he followed Thomas into the house.

Retribution for the affair seemed mercifully just. Mistress Fuller belied her frail body and was fully recovered the next day but Thomas caught a heavy cold and went about the house sneezing and sniffing. He had clearly had a good fright at the near outcome of his prank — which in itself had failed completely. The windmill continued to run unmolested.

On the morning after the rescue Sarah

announced her intention of riding to the village to find Master Fuller and tell him that his sister had suffered no mishap. Word had been sent the day before that the water trial had not proved fatal but that his sister would be kept at Banks House overnight.

"There is, of course, one thing you seem to have forgotten," Father O'Brien said thoughtfully as Sarah turned to leave the room.

"What do you mean?" Thomas and Sarah spoke together.

"You may have saved the old woman's actual life but the life she knows now may be finished."

"Go on," Thomas said thickly.

"The trial for witchcraft by water has two possible outcomes. Either the accused sinks and drowns, in which case she is declared to be innocent, or she swims and is saved. She is then declared to be a witch and is hanged or burned."

"Yes, that's common knowledge but what has it to do with Mistress Fuller? The trial was a fake, as everyone must realise, and she was drowning when Tom rescued her. So far as Sir George is concerned, the whole thing was a failure." Sarah sounded puzzled.

"For Sir George, yes, but the point is this," Father O'Brien said patiently. "The old woman did not drown — therefore she has been proven to be a witch! It may seem nonsense to you but some of the villagers will reason in this way, so don't be too hasty in sending her home."

"All the people at the poolside yesterday were acting very strangely," Stephen said thoughtfully.

"Well, let's hope their womenfolk have talked some sense during the night then!" Sarah said briskly, once more making for the door.

"All the same, I think I had better come with you, just in case there is any trouble." Stephen's mind went back to the sullenness of the crowd the previous day.

"Oh, come for the ride if you want! I'm quite certain no one will harm me, no matter what mischief they may mean to do Mistress Fuller, though as she has been sick nurse and midwife to them for many years they will surely not abandon her now."

6

SARAH proved to be right in the first part, if not in the second. The women bobbed their usual curtsies and the men touched their foreheads, even though everyone must have known what her errand in the village was. There was no sign of Master Fuller anywhere, so Sarah led the way to a small tumble-down cottage at the far end of the village. There was no one outside but a thin curl of smoke above the chimney indicated that someone was inside.

"Do you mean to go in?" Stephen asked, for some reason uneasy.

"Certainly I do!" Sarah called a young boy to hold the horses.

At first no one answered her knocking but finally Master Fuller did come to the door and, opening it a crack, peered out.

"My lady! 'Tis better you don't come here!" He started to close the door.

But Sarah had one hand firmly on it. "Why?"

"The whole village is saying that my sister is proved to be a witch. They say it doesn't matter that 'is lordship saved 'er. They don't want 'er to come back to the village — ever."

"That's pure nonsense! Oh, let me come in, will you? We can't stand discussing it in the road!"

The old man reluctantly opened the door and they stepped into the one small, dark room of which the downstairs of the cottage consisted. The old man pushed a sleeping black cat off the only chair and begged Sarah to sit. Stephen found himself too tall to stand upright under the low ceiling and stood awkwardly, head bowed, behind her.

Sarah looked at the cat with a smile. "I suppose they are saying that he is one of her familiars!" she remarked jokingly.

The old man shuffled his feet uncomfortably. "Yes, my lady, they be saying just that."

"Everyone really believes that Mistress Fuller was being tried for witchcraft?"

"Oh, yes, my lady. You see, she has the second sight and can see into the future. She foretells fortunes for people and the whole village knows this. But seeing into the future still don't make 'er a witch!" he added stubbornly.

"No, of course it doesn't," Sarah said soothingly and added more to Stephen: "Oh, God, what a mess! And seeing that the trouble was of our making, I think . . . " A loud knocking cut her short.

Stephen stiffened and his right hand reached for his sword. The old man looked terrified and he made no move to open the door. He looked at Sarah as if for support. Sarah clearly had no intention of dodging the issue and calmly told him to open it.

"Go on, Master Fuller!" She leant forward and gave him a little shove.

The knock sounded again, louder and longer.

"Coming, coming!" the old man mumbled, shuffling to the door and opening it wide.

Sir George Fanworth and his steward strode into the room, making it seem uncomfortably overcrowded. Sir George stared at Sarah and Stephen for a moment, then, remembering his manners, he bowed.

"I might have thought to find you here meddling, sweetheart!" he said shortly.

Sarah looked at him with dislike but answered calmly: "We came to bring Master Fuller a message, that is all."

"Yes? And I have a message for him too! Master Steward, give him the eviction notice!"

The steward stepped forward and Stephen recognised the big man who had asked if he were the new Commissioner of Sewers on the evening of his arrival. The old man took the piece of paper but did not look at it.

"What do you mean, 'eviction notice'?" Sarah tried to see what was written on the paper.

"You at least can read, sweetheart! It means that I want Master Fuller and his sister out of the cottage immediately."

"You can't mean that! Why, in heaven's name?"

"Really, madam, I don't think it is any of your business!"

"Nevertheless I am asking you why you are putting these old people out of their home — such as it is. You, as landlord, should be ashamed of it!"

Sir George looked mockingly at her. "Exactly so! I am ashamed of it and mean to have it pulled down and rebuilt. The new cottage will of course be far superior to this one, and I fear Master Fuller will never be able to pay the increased rent. He doesn't do enough work now to merit this one."

"If you are going to have this cottage pulled down you should provide another one for them!" There was an angry edge to Sarah's voice.

"I have already told you! Master Fuller and his sister do not pay their rent regularly, therefore I have no obligation to them!" Sir George was also beginning to lose his temper.

"No obligation indeed! Have you no heart?"

Sir George flushed but before he could make a retort Master Fuller asked pitifully: "What can I do if we leave here? We have nowhere to go and my sister is too old to tramp the roads."

"From what I hear, your sister has already left the village," Sir George said meaningfully.

"Yes, thanks to you!" Sarah broke

in wrathfully. "However, stop worrying, Master Fuller. I am sure my brother will be able to find somewhere for you to live at Banks House."

"Temporary accommodation only, sweetheart!"

Sarah bit her lip as this shot went home but she kept silent and Sir George went on: "By the way, where is your brother today? Surely he should not be sending you to run his errands?"

"My brother . . . " Sarah began furiously when Stephen intervened.

Until now he had stood, a silent spectator, in the background but Sir George's last piece of rudeness was too much. He stepped forward, his hand still resting on the hilt of his sword. Even with his head bowed, he was able to look down on Sir George.

"I think you are being insulting to the lady, sir! Lord Gerton is at home indisposed — the result of bravely preventing a murder. You at least should be grateful to him!"

Sir George's eyes dropped before Stephen's blazing blue ones but he held his ground.

"If Lord Gerton did not meddle in the concerns of others there would be less trouble all round," he asserted.

By this time Stephen was very angry, perhaps more angry than the other two. "And if you acted in a more humane manner there would also be less trouble!" he said frankly, with less than his usual caution.

"Another champion entering the lists!" Sir George sneered.

"It should not be necessary for me to have to champion Lady Sarah. That, I believe, is your duty as you are shortly to marry her!" Stephen spoke with sudden coldness.

Sir George turned a fine burgundy colour and his hand flew to his sword. "Are you suggesting — "

Sarah rose deliberately from her chair. "Sir George! My lord! I don't think any of us have manners to quarrel like this in Master Fuller's home — for it is his private home until he is forced out of it. Also Lord Ansell is my brother's guest and mine." She turned to the old man who was standing back against the wall looking completely dazed. "Master

Fuller, Lord Gerton will have a cart sent this afternoon for your possessions. Do you pack your things now."

Sarah would have left the room but Sir George blocked the way.

"As Lord Ansell so kindly pointed out, I am soon to marry you, sweetheart. Therefore you should honour me — not gainsay my orders! I have told Master Fuller and his sister to take themselves right off my property. I would thank you to leave my arrangements to me!"

Sarah stared at him, eyes blazing, but she still held her temper under control.

"I am not yet your wife, sir, and until I am I shall continue to honour my brother's wishes! Now if you would allow Lord Ansell and myself to pass, please."

Sir George moved aside and Sarah swept out of the low doorway. Stephen and Sir George looked at one another in mutual dislike for a moment, then Stephen, with a slight bow, followed Sarah out.

For all his lean build, Stephen possessed great wiry strength and he tossed Sarah up into the saddle as if she were a child. Their moment of contact as he lifted her lasted only a few seconds but it was enough for Sarah to feel the wrath still vibrant within him.

As she gathered up her reins she smiled down at him and said with more warmth than usual: "Thank you for championing our cause, cousin, but you should not have quarrelled with Sir George — he is a bad man to cross."

"As I'm unlikely to meet the man again, it hardly matters. But you did not exactly soothe your prospective husband yourself, my lady!" Stephen echoed her smile.

Sir George, emerging from the cottage, though he did not hear the words, saw the smiles and was in no way soothed.

Thomas met Stephen and Sarah in the hall on their return, anxious to know what had kept them for so long.

"Sir George has evicted the Fullers from their cottage and he does not take kindly to our rehousing them here! The villagers have also rejected Mistress Fuller as Father O'Brien said they might, so we must find somewhere for them, Tom."

"Can you take over another man's tenants?" Stephen asked, mildly interested.

"If they've been evicted I don't see why not," but Thomas sounded uncertain.

"Would you have us abandon them?" Sarah demanded coldly.

"By no means — considering that it is your fault they are in their present trouble!" Stephen said bluntly.

"You know Tom only meant to frighten Sir George into abandoning the windmill."

"I know you both acted in good faith but without enough forethought. It was a good try but unfortunately it misfired."

Seeing the colour rising in Sarah's cheeks, Thomas said hastily: "Where should we put them? There are a couple of rooms at the back of the stables which could be made habitable, I think."

Leaving his cousins to arrange housing for the Fullers, Stephen went upstairs, hoping that his aunt was strong enough for a visit. He found her lying propped up against the pillows and looking extremely bored. Her expression brightened instantly on seeing her visitor.

"Stephen! I am so glad you have come

to see me! Perhaps now I can get to the bottom of what has been going on since I took to my bed — for something has been going on, I'm sure. Your uncle just hedges and probably would get it all wrong anyway!"

"I'm glad I find you sufficiently recovered to take an interest in family gossip! But how are you, Aunt? You had us all very worried!" Stephen picked up a chair and placed it next to the bed.

Mrs Perrington reached out and patted his arm. "No need to worry about me, dear boy — I'm a lot tougher than I look! But I'll rest easier if I know what has been going on. And no hedging, mind!"

Stephen obliged, leaving out only the details of his quarrel with Sir George.

Mrs Perrington watched him closely, sensing disquiet behind the account he strove to keep light-hearted. "What fear you, Stephen? — that young Gerton has been dabbling in Black Magic?"

Stephen got up and folded his arms over the back of the chair.

"No, not now, though I did wonder at first. Now I am sure it was just a silly, misguided prank but I have the feeling that Gerton, and Sarah too, are somehow in league with the villagers over the sabotaging of Sir George's drainage works. Sarah swears that her brother is not the leader, in fact has nothing to do with the gang."

"Don't you believe her?"

"Yes, I think I do, though obviously Gerton's sympathies lie with the villagers. But I am quite sure they both know who the Black Monk is."

"That would hardly be surprising when they have lived here all their lives, just about."

"True. And as long as they leave it at that there is no harm done but if they meddle deeper there will be trouble. Sir George has already contacted the Commissioner of Sewers."

"I should imagine they have far bigger troubles to keep them occupied than to come investigating some minor landowner's petty complaints."

"Sarah said something like that." Stephen straightened himself and stood restlessly playing with the bed hangings.

Mrs Perrington lay watching him.

After a pause she asked: "What really is disturbing you, Stephen?"

He looked down at her. "I think Sarah is storing up trouble for herself. The man is a fanatic about his schemes and here she is thwarting him as often as she can. Only weeks before the wedding too. I don't imagine he would be an easy man to live with at the best of times, and continually crossed . . . " Stephen shrugged.

His aunt frowned. "I think you are worrying needlessly," she said slowly. "Sarah is quite old enough to know what she is about."

"Perhaps, but could you not point out to her that a little prudence where Sir George is concerned might be in order?"

"I could, but would I be in order? Sarah must, after all, have chosen Sir George as her husband — I am sure her father would not have forced her to marry anyone against her will, so stop worrying, Stephen. Once she is wed I am sure Sarah will become a dutiful wife."

Probably beaten into being one, Stephen thought sadly. The old Earl hadn't used brute force but he had used the next best way — the most certain way. For an instant Stephen thought of confiding Sarah's dilemma to their aunt but he quickly discarded the idea. There was nothing she could do and Sarah would not thank him for the interference. Besides it would greatly upset Aunt Bess.

He mustered a smile. "In other words, it is none of my affair! Rest assured, Aunt, I have no intention of meddling — I'll leave that pastime for others!"

"Unfortunately there is not much else to do in this isolated spot. I quite agree that the sooner Sarah is married and Thomas takes over the control of his estate the better it will be for both of them. It is a great pity this house is so far from town. A large circle of friends would go a long way towards keeping them out of mischief."

"Yes, it's a case of idle hands maketh no good work!"

Mrs Perrington looked at him shrewdly. "And I have kept you idle overlong, I think?"

Stephen could not deny it. "I am

anxious to get home now, yes, but only now that I know all is well again with you, Aunt. Promise me you will get Uncle to take you home as soon as you are fit to travel?"

"As soon as I am ready. Now we are so near to Sarah's wedding I think we could stay for that, don't you?"

"No I don't! Most decidedly not! Another few weeks would bring you right to the very brink of winter — the time of damp and fog. Why, it might be complete disaster for you to travel then."

"We will have to consult the physician about it, won't we?" Mrs Perrington clearly did not intend to give in without a fight but she abruptly changed the subject. "And what about Mistress Lucy? Shouldn't you have been visiting her instead of kicking your heels round here?"

Stephen had been asking himself the same question for some days and found no answer. What he felt for Lucy he was not sure but he did know he had no wish to hurt her. The only way to know her better was to be with her, yet if she mistook his interest for something deeper she might suffer.

"I think you are probably right, Aunt," he said slowly. "Lucy is delightful . . . and yet I somehow feel so old compared to her."

Mrs Perrington heard the hesitancy in his explanation but ignored it. "What nonsense you talk, Stephen! The girl must be all of eighteen and you are what — twenty-six, twenty-seven? The gap is tiny compared to that of some marriages."

"Yes, but I have no wish for a marriage of mere convenience — I saw too many of those at Court."

"Well, you won't find love by sitting about here!"

"True. I have promised to visit her on my way home."

"And when is that?"

"Tomorrow morning, all being well."

7

THOMAS nursed his cold indoors for the rest of the day and was considerably better by the time the Comte arrived to sup with them. The event of a visitor cheered them all up though Stephen's enjoyment was slightly marred by the shower of compliments de Verais poured on Sarah. She responded gracefully and with every sign of enjoyment. It was a good thing Sir George had not been invited, Stephen thought glumly. Watching his cousin's animated face, he felt a stab of foreboding — oh, God, it just needed the girl to fall madly in love with the Comte before her wedding.

Sarah however seemed to have the situation well under control. At the end of the meal she announced that she was leaving the gentlemen to their wine and cards while she went to sit with her aunt.

"Lucky aunt!" said de Verais, bowing

low over her hand. "Cannot I persuade you that our need is greater than hers — "

"Oh, no, sir!" Sarah said with a little curtsy. "Why, as soon as the cards are dealt you will forget that I exist!"

"Ah! But the cards are not yet dealt. Nor need they be! A game of cards would be a very small thing to forgo in order to keep the company of such a beautiful lady!"

For a moment Sarah looked nonplussed. She was slightly flushed and the compliments had given sparkle to her eyes. She is beautiful, Stephen thought, surprised. If she stays there will be trouble, no matter what Aunt says. Silently he tried to will her to leave the room.

Sarah responded unconsciously. She curtsied again. "You forget, sir, that my aunt has been lying alone for most of the day," she pointed out gently. "She will be waiting most eagerly for the supper gossip!"

De Verais bowed his defeat. "Of course. It is unforgivable of me to try to detain you." He said humbly. "My felicitations to Madame Perrington."

Stephen, who was nearest, opened the door for Sarah and heaved a mental sigh of relief as he closed it behind her. A few minutes later Father O'Brien also withdrew, leaving the four men to settle down to their game in the small parlour.

The hour was growing late when Stephen thought he heard the sound of hoofbeats. Thomas, perhaps because of his stuffy head, seemed to hear nothing and calmly played on. A few minutes later Stephen knew he had been right — there came a loud knocking on the front door.

Thomas laid down his cards with a sigh. "Who, at this time?" he asked carelessly but Stephen caught his sudden tension.

A few moments later Burnet ushered in Sir George — obviously angry, though this was quickly hidden, and taken aback to find Thomas had a visitor. His bow to Thomas and Stephen was correct, but deeper to the Comte.

"This is an unlooked-for pleasure, sir! I had not thought to find you here."

"Nor I you, sir!" returned de Verais, puzzled as much by the sudden general atmosphere of wariness as by Sir George's strange hour of arrival.

Sir George turned to Thomas. "Had I known you were entertaining, Lord Gerton, I should have not come seeking your help." For once he sounded diffident.

"Our help?"

"The Black Monk has been seen again on my property tonight. I thought if you and Lord Ansell would kindly join me an all-out search might settle the matter once and forever."

"Why not? You have an extra man!" de Verais pointed out.

"I thank you, sir!"

"You will not go out tonight, Gerton?" Mr Perrington asked anxiously.

"Good God, Uncle, I only have a cold in the head!"

"Nevertheless it would be most unwise in my opinion. Look what your aunt has suffered from taking a simple chill."

"My cold is really nothing, sir, so there is no need to worry — I shall come to no harm in that direction, I assure you! I cannot ignore a neighbour in need, besides, would you have me stay safely indoors while my guests ride out! You will come, Ansell?"

"Naturally!" Stephen said drily. He looked at Sir George but the man refused to meet his eye.

It was a pleasant night, with a quarter-moon behind a haze to relieve them of the necessity of carrying lanterns. There was a strong smell of rain in the still air and a heavy silence brooded everywhere. Stephen rode in the direction he had been allotted for as near half an hour as he could judge. By that time he had no idea where he was and all he could do was to turn round and hope he was heading back towards Banks House. There was no sign of a single living creature. Somewhere a marsh bird screeched, then was sharply quiet, leaving the silence more profound than before.

Suddenly sniffing, Stephen thought he could smell the salty decay of the marsh. If he could find the edge of it he was certain he could find his way home — provided he did not fall into a bog on the way. The ground at present was hard and he made his horse keep a fair pace.

Without warning Land-Lubber stopped of his own accord, so sharply that Stephen, whose thoughts were miles away, was thrown forward onto the horse's neck. Putting back his ears, Land-Lubber whinnied softly. Almost beneath the horse's hoofs an answering neigh came out of the darkness. Peering down, Stephen saw that his horse had stopped at the edge of a wide, deep dyke.

Stephen slipped out of the saddle and, looping up the reins over Land-Lubber's neck, left him standing while he scrambled down the bank into the dyke. The bottom was muddy but there was only a trickle of water at one side. A horse was standing tethered to a bush which grew in a break in the far bank — probably the point through which the animal had entered the dyke. By touch more than by sight Stephen ascertained that the animal was fully saddled but seemingly alone.

Doubtlessly the owner would be returning soon and Stephen made up his mind to wait for him. At first he decided to remain at the bottom of the dyke with the horse, then he realised that his own horse at the top of the bank would give his presence away to anyone not actually down in the dyke. As silently as he could he climbed the steep side of the dyke, and led Land-Lubber some way from the edge into a group of trees. Beyond these he could see a silhouette of a more regular shape than that of trees and realised that he must have come up on the far side of Banks Priory. Getting home would be easy from here.

A slight sound made him spin round. He could easily make out a dark figure walking across the open ground towards the dyke where the horse was tethered. There was no attempt at concealment, so Stephen guessed that his own presence was not suspected.

It was now or never, Stephen decided. Throwing away all caution, he sprinted across the field and hurled himself at the dark figure. As the distance closed between them Stephen saw the pale blob of a face surrounded by a black hood or cowl turn towards him. Unfortunately, in the uncertain light he miscalculated, or the stranger dodged at the last second, for all his outstretched hands encountered was the man's hood. The force of Stephen's tackle caused him to overbalance and his fingers hardly had time to close on the material before he found himself crashing down.

The next moment he was lying full length on the ground, alone and half winded. A squelching sound nearby told him that the man had escaped down into the dyke. As he fought for breath, the blackness spinning round him, Stephen thought he heard someone call: "Au revoir, monsieur!" but by the time his lungs were again filled with air all he could hear was fading hoofbeats.

Cursing himself soundly, Stephen sat up and then got slowly to his feet. He was unhurt but he felt he had come out of the encounter very poorly. Feeling round for his hat which had come off when he fell, he realised that he was still holding some strands of material or hair. On an impulse he twisted the strands into his hatband. It was possible he might be able to guess the identity of the man from them. He looked into the dyke but it was too dark to see if the man had left anything behind. With a shrug Stephen turned and walked back across the field to where Land-Lubber was patiently waiting.

He led the horse out from beneath the trees and fumbled for a moment getting his foot into the stirrup. He sprang upwards and was almost level with the saddle when he noticed a flash away to his left and simultaneously an explosion broke over him. Something smashed into his leg, knocking his foot from the stirrup, and for the second time that night he went crashing to the ground. This time the starlight faded into unrelieved blackness. The minutes ticked by and he made no move to rise.

Presently a dark form crept up to Stephen's inert body and someone tried to peer at his face in the dim light. Apparently satisfied, the figure stole away into the darkness.

It seemed to Stephen that he floated in blackness for a very long time. During a brief period of half-consciousness he heard a mumble of voices around him. One clearer than the rest asked: "Dear God, is he dead too?" Stephen thought it was Sarah's voice and he tried to open his eyes but the lids were too heavy. Then he was being moved and the sounds faded.

When the darkness receded Stephen felt more comfortable. However his respite did not last long, for someone poured a choking liquid into his mouth and urged him to "Hold on!"

For a moment Stephen was able to get his eyes open. Surrounding him were several faces, lit in a blaze of candle light. He knew he should recognise them but there was no time — hold on was just what he could not do. There was a stab of pain in his leg so fierce that he was sent rushing back into the well of darkness. He heard a gasp of agony and as the sound followed him down into the blackness he knew it was his own.

After that he continued to float for an endless period. Mostly he was suspended in utter blackness but at times he seemed to hear sounds around him. Voices came and went. He heard the howl of wind in the rigging and the sound of water slapping against the hull. What he was doing at sea and where he was bound for he had not the slightest idea, nor could he be bothered to work it out. Later, when all was quiet, he wondered if there had been a battle which was now over, though he could not remember any fighting or ordering out of the cannon. Here something stirred in his memory. Cannon caused flashes of fire and explosions — vaguely he could remember a flash and an explosion. Also something hitting his leg.

His next thought made him lie very still. He had seen cannon balls rip the limbs from men — had he had his leg torn off? It seemed to ache from hip to ankle but he had heard of men experiencing pain in limbs they no longer possessed. Had that happened to him? He forced his eyes open.

Stephen's surroundings were not what he expected to see. Instead of a cramped, low-beamed ship's cabin and a narrow bunk, he found he was lying in a big bed. The hangings were drawn back and he saw that the room was his bedchamber at Banks House. A candle, low in its holder, flickered on a table but the room was full of the grey light of a rain swept dawn.

So sea, storm and battle were just a dream — however the pain in his leg was not. He struggled to sit up and at his grunt of pain, Sarah, who had been standing wearily looking out of the tightly closed casement, turned swiftly round. For an instant Stephen saw the blank despair in her eyes — she might have been crying — then the look was gone.

"Oh, Stephen, I'm glad you've woken up at last. We were beginning to think you would never recover consciousness."

"The physician's potion must have been powerful! How long have I been out?" he asked weakly.

"More than a day and a night."

"I was dreaming. I dreamed . . . " The effort of talking and keeping his eyes open was too much. He felt more tired than he had ever been in his life, even after fighting storm and shipwreck. It would be easier to go back to dreaming. He let his eyelids droop.

"Stephen!" Sarah seized his wrist. "Stephen, wake up! You must not sleep again until you have taken some nourishment. Is the light hurting your eyes? I shouldn't have opened the curtains."

Sarah's voice sounded urgent. Summoning up the strength, he looked at her. "No, my eyes don't hurt," he began slowly and stopped.

"But your leg does?"

Stephen nodded, his eyes focused on Sarah's face.

Suddenly she read his mute appeal.

"Don't worry, cousin, your leg will be all right," she said gently. "It has a hole in it but the bone is not broken. It is because you have lost so much blood that you feel so ill. And if you don't have something to sustain you you really will slip away for good. We have been keeping some broth hot for you ever since the physician got the bullet out. Please try to keep awake while I fetch some.

"Oh, go and get it then!" Stephen was too relieved to argue.

Sarah returned presently and began to feed him with mouthfuls of bread soaked in the broth. Stephen felt foolish but he was too weak to protest. He had little appetite; however he took the contents of the bowl obediently.

"Now you can sleep as much as you

like," Sarah remarked, straightening the covers. "Would you like the curtains closing?"

"No, thank you, cousin."

Stephen lay flat on his back watching her through half closed lids. Sarah looked very tired but she was also subtly altered — almost as if something within her had been rekindled. Stephen remembered his worries about de Verais.

"Are your brother and de Verais all right?" he asked.

"Oh, yes. Neither came to any harm at all. The Comte was wonderful! It was he who found you, fetched help and controlled the bleeding until the physician arrived. Without him you would assuredly be dead."

Stephen heard the warmth in her voice and wished he had not asked the question. He changed the subject abruptly.

"How long have you been watching over me?"

"Since midnight or thereabouts. We have all been taking turns to sit with you. We even had the greatest difficulty in restraining Aunt Bess from rising from her bed to take a turn!"

"You must be very tired with two patients to attend. I'm sorry."

"It is hardly your fault!"

"Well, in a way it is. I found the Black Monk last night, or rather the night before, but I let him slip through my fingers!"

"You actually saw the man?"

"I literally tangled with him! But at the crucial moment I fell flat on my face and he escaped."

"How frustrating! Did you recognise him?"

The question was natural enough but Sarah was too tired to act sufficiently interested in something to which Stephen guessed she already knew the answer.

"No, it was far too dark," he said slowly. "But we have learned one thing, though — the man is a murderer and a good shot."

"Whatever do you mean?" He had Sarah's interest now.

"It stands to reason that he must have shot me. And if I had not been in the act of mounting my horse the shot would have got me in the head or the chest instead of in the leg."

Sarah stared at him open-mouthed, as if she would protest, then she pulled herself together and said quietly: "The man has never been known to use violence to people. But this is not the time to go into the question of who shot you. You must rest and I am tiring you by talking."

She looked out of the window at the falling rain and added: "Just give thanks that you and the Comte both wandered off course towards each other and that he heard the shot . . . "

Looking up, Stephen saw a strange look in his cousin's eyes, then her light-coloured lashes formed a veil of raw silk and it was gone. Certain that his fears that the girl was falling in love had been substantiated, he closed his eyes with an exhausted sigh.

8

A FEW days later Sir George, apparently having heard that Stephen was sufficiently recovered to receive visitors, arrived to beg Stephen's pardon for leading him into harm — an apology that Stephen felt was mere form and not in the least genuine. Sir George had scarcely seated himself when Sarah ushered in the Comte de Verais and the two eldest Gleeson sisters.

"If only I had been nearer to you it might never have happened," de Verais said ruefully.

His words held far more warmth than Sir George's had and to cover his embarrassment Stephen asked: "You didn't see who did it, I suppose?"

"Unfortunately not."

Everyone seemed to have his own idea about it and under cover of the ensuing argument Stephen turned to Lucy.

"Once again you had to wait in vain for me. You will think I am never coming."

"At first I did wonder . . . " Lucy began honestly, then smiled at him. "But now all you must think about is getting well, then perhaps . . . "

They were interrupted by Sir George's saying loudly: "Just find the Black Monk and ask him!"

"But you know the man never uses violence," Thomas protested. "Besides he had no reason to shoot Ansell — he had got clean away in the dark and could be fairly certain of remaining unrecognised."

"What about the time John Carr was shot dead?" Sir George asked brutally. "No other murderer has ever been found."

Sarah stiffened instantly. "You have yet to prove it! More like it was one of your men who shot him!"

"I told you before — my men carried no firearms that night." Sir George looked slyly at Sarah. "Obviously the silly boy must have provoked 'Prior Brulac' in some way and was killed for his pains."

Sarah went very white and for a moment Stephen thought she was going to say something she would regret, but de Verais, who had been looking out of the window, turned round and re-entered the argument.

"Peace, friends, peace! Are we not here to cheer up Lord Ansell? Certainly we should not be fighting round him! I think you were mistaken for the saboteur himself, milord, or mayhap even for an unwelcome lover!" He smiled mischievously down at Stephen.

Stephen turned somewhat pink at this sally but the Comte's words had the desired effect for both Sarah and Thomas gave involuntary hoots of laughter.

Mr Perrington, who had come into the room unnoticed, slapped his thigh in delight. "That's it, of course! Some irate father or husband thought you had come avisiting his daughter or wife, and decided to take quick action! I must tell your Aunt that!"

They left it at that but the question returned to Stephen when his guests had departed. He could not answer it and his sense of baffled rage grew. He should be back at Deeford working, not lying here helpless. Stephen twisted impatiently in the big bed, another thought coming to him. Because of his accident the

Comte now had an excellent excuse for visiting Banks House and seeing Sarah. Sir George would be honour bound to call often too and if he came to suspect there was anything between Sarah and de Verais Sarah's troubles would be magnified a hundred-fold. Knowing the man's ready temper, Stephen guessed Sir George would not hesitate to call the Comte out. De Verais was, no doubt, a fine swordsman, but Sir George? It might be a way out for Sarah, but what of Gerton's estate?

That night Stephen did not sleep well. His leg pained him and his head ached. When he did finally drop off to sleep it was to dream that Sir George and the Comte were fighting a duel. Both men were dripping blood but neither gained a deciding thrust. The fight went on and on, interspersed with oddments of other dreams, and there was still no victor when Stephen woke up.

He wakened feeling unwell and as the day wore on he felt worse.

The physician, calling on a routine visit, looked at Stephen's leg and, finding the wound cleanly scabbed over, decided

Stephen must have a fever, but as the days went by and his course of bleeding and purging only left Stephen weaker and the fever unabated Sarah and Morris became steadily more worried.

"I'm mortal certain the wound be poisoned, my lady. I've seen them go like that before," Morris said to Sarah one evening as they attempted to settle Stephen for the night.

She looked at him with a worried frown.

"I think you are probably right. Yet the physician is so sure that it is not the wound."

"Perhaps he hasn't seen as many shot wounds as I 'ave. He be only a physician, not a surgeon!" Morris said dourly. He had served with one armed force or another since boyhood and being a gentleman's body-servant was a tame venture made palatable only by his liking for his present master.

"Nevertheless he should know if a wound is poisoned or not," Sarah said unhappily. "It is not easy to tell a learned doctor that he is wrong."

"If the learned doctor does not change

his mind his lordship will be dead," Morris said bluntly and, picking up the bowl and linen with which he had mopped his master's sweat drenched face, he marched uncompromisingly into the dressing-closet.

Next morning, as she attempted to busy herself in the dairy, Sarah's thoughts turned over and over like cream in the churn. Just how did you convince a physician that his diagnosis and treatment were wrong when you had no medical knowledge yourself? An hour later, and no nearer the answer, she became aware that she was no longer alone. Mistress Fuller had slipped unnoticed into the still-room and was standing just inside the door. How long she had been there Sarah had no idea.

Mistress Fuller bobbed a stiff curtsy when she saw that Sarah had noticed her.

"Lord Ansell is not well, my lady?" The words were more a statement than a question.

Sarah looked at the bowl of cream between her hands. "Lord Ansell is dying," she said slowly, knowing it to be the truth.

"Let me see 'im, my lady. I'm well skilled in the arts of 'ealing."

"You? What could you do?" Sarah looked at her doubtfully.

The old woman stared steadily back. "I know most of what there is to know about 'erbs and plant extracts. No one can know all. I know too of treating poisoned wounds."

For a moment Sarah did not answer. The old woman was thought to be a witch and one of the reasons for this belief was that she performed miraculous cures. There could be little danger in letting her see Stephen — she was not likely to harm him as he had helped to save her life. Doctor Somers would be appalled but perhaps he need not know. All his reputed knowledge was doing Stephen no good and there was a slim chance that Mistress Fuller, if she were skilled enough, might succeed where the physician had failed.

Aloud she said: "Come with me now, if you will."

She led Mistress Fuller up a back stairs and into Stephen's bedchamber. For a long moment the old woman stood by the bed where Stephen, shrunk now to skeleton thinness, tossed uncomprehendingly beneath the covers that Morris struggled to keep over him.

Morris gave the old woman a swift look of surprised suspicion when Sarah led her into the room but he did not demur when she asked him to remove the bandages from his master's leg. One glance at Stephen's leg, which in the night had begun to swell and had turned a hideous reddish purple round the wound, cast out any doubts Sarah and Morris might have had about the wound being poisoned.

Mistress Fuller clearly had no doubts either.

"The poison is far advanced but I think there be yet time," she murmured half to herself, and louder: "I will be back before the light fades. See that there is a good fire burning." With that she was gone.

Stephen awoke from a restless sleep about mid-afternoon.

If possible, he felt more ill than before, but for the time being at least his mind was clear. Up till now he had followed Doctor Somer's lead and refused to believe that anything was wrong with the wound in his leg. Now the pain was such that he knew he and the physician were wrong. For the first time he wished the ball had smashed through the bone and the physician had had to amputate his leg. It was a bit late but now, while his faculties were clear, he was going to tell the old blockhead to stop taking his blood and to take off his leg instead.

Stephen did not see Mistress Fuller come into the room with Sarah, nor did he see her go softly over to the fire which was blazing in the hearth and put something into the hottest coals, so he was surprised when her small wizened face suddenly appeared next to him.

"Will it please your lordship to drink this?" Timidly she held out a beaker to him.

Sarah, who had also crossed to the bed, slid her arm under his pillow and, raising his head, held the beaker to his lips.

"Drink it, Stephen," she commanded. "Mistress Fuller has come to see if her knowledge of herbs cannot help you more than the physician's treatment."

It could hardly do less, he thought, but to be treated by a witch was scarcely more propitious. He had no strength to protest, besides he was thirsty, so he drank the sickly-smelling brew. The taste was even more foul than the smell and he choked over the last mouthful. However he had taken enough to satisfy Mistress Fuller for she signed to Sarah to set the beaker down.

Before long a wonderful numbing lassitude crept over him. He hardly noticed that Morris was gently unwinding the bandage from his swollen leg. The pain which had tormented him for so many days was fading away. He watched without interest when Mistress Fuller went to the fire and removed a knife from the coals. For an instant the long thin blade glowed red hot as she held it in one monkey-small hand. She said something to Morris and Stephen protested feebly as he felt the big hands grip him firmly. The old woman crossed the floor to stand next to the bed, knife in hand, and, for all the numbness clouding his brain, Stephen realised what she meant to do.

"Oh, no!" he gasped, knowing that the words would be ineffective.

He shut his eyes and grasped at the

nearest thing, unaware that it was his cousin's wrist as she leant over to hold him. He did not see the old woman thrust the knife at a slight angle deeply into his leg next to the scab, twisting it a little as she did so, but he felt it. His grip closed convulsively, then he slid into merciful unconsciousness.

Sarah, feeling nearly as faint as her cousin, watched with fascination the stream of poison welling out from the knife wound. Mistress Fuller calmly began to clean the abscess with a distillation she had brought in a flask with her. Only when she was satisfied that the abscess was clean did she pack the opening with salve and tell Morris to bandage it.

"Wash it out night and morning with that and pack it with salve," she instructed Morris, indicating the flask and jar.

Her still bright old eyes darted to Sarah's pale face.

"'E'll do fine now, my lady. A life for a life." Her lips parted in a black-toothed smile. "'E'll live to win the day for ee yet!"

Sarah looked down at her cousin's unconscious face, now almost as white as the frills of his nightshirt. A life for a life. She hoped the old woman was right.

* * *

It seemed that she was. Stephen remained in a deep drugged sleep all night and throughout most of the next day. He awoke at last feeling very much better. He was exceedingly weak and his leg was sore but the fever and the excruciating pain were gone. When Doctor Somers called he found his patient so much better that he pronounced him well on the way to recovery and did not even ask to have Stephen's leg unbandaged. Sarah neglected to tell him that the leg had been lanced.

A few mornings later Sarah came into Stephen's bedchamber with a pile of clean linen for his bed. Her sleeves were pushed up to the elbows and as she set down the linen he noticed a band of bruising on her right wrist.

"Devil take it! Have you been fighting

with Sir George?" Stephen asked, staring at her wrist.

"Fighting with George? No. Why?"

"Who gave you those terrible bruises on your wrist then?"

Sarah glanced at the yellowish purple marks and grinned mockingly at him.

"You did, cousin!" she told him jeeringly.

"Good God! When?" Stephen was appalled.

"Don't look so stricken!" Sarah said more gently, sorry that she had teased him. "You didn't know what you were doing. When Mistress Fuller lanced your leg you needed something to grab hold of. I happened to be in your way, that is all."

"I'm sorry." Stephen took her hand and turned it palm out. The marks of his fingers were even more clearly defined on the soft inside of her wrist. "God, how I must have hurt you!" he said contritely.

Sarah flushed and tried to pull her hand away but Stephen's long thin fingers held it firmly as he looked at a narrow scar which ran from just above his bruises to vanish in the ruffles at her elbow. He had seen many such scars but only on men never on a woman before.

"What a virago you are, cousin! I see you indulge in the manly sport of swordplay!" It was Stephen's turn to tease.

In one swift agitated movement Sarah jerked her hand away and pulled down her sleeve.

"Please forget you saw it. I'm in enough trouble for my hoydenish ways as it is."

"Sir George does not seem to mind them?"

"Should he — he's no gentleman!"

"And yet you still mean to go through with the wedding?"

"What do you mean 'still'? I told you I would never go back on my word!"

"But now you are in love with another man, aren't you?" he asked softly.

Stephen saw the colour flood into Sarah's face before she turned swiftly away. "Nevertheless I can't break my vow, not for love, not for anything," she said in a stifled voice.

"Then let me give you a piece of

cousinly advice," Stephen said slowly, bracing himself.

"Go on." Sarah did not turn round.

"Be careful how you go with de Verais when Sir George is around. If you let Sir George suspect you are in love with someone he will make life hell on earth for you once you are wed."

For several moments there was absolute silence, then Sarah said quietly: "Thank you, cousin. I had thought of that and I will take great care not to let the Comte flirt with me when Sir George is here. I agree — he must not think that I could be in love with another man. He knows my feelings towards him will never change."

"Forgive me. I would not have spoken so frankly about your private affairs if it hadn't been a matter of urgency." Stephen eyed Sarah's stiffened back uneasily.

She swung round. The colour had died from her face leaving it pallid and frozen. Her eyes held a strange expression.

"Damn you, Stephen! Why did you have to come here and get mixed up in our troubles!"

Abruptly she left the room.

Eventually came the day when Doctor Somers gave Stephen permission to leave his bed. The experiment was not all Stephen would have wished for. His body felt as if it were made of cold pudding and he could barely hobble as far as the nearest chair.

"Don't fret, my lord," Morris said cheeringly. "After all the blood you lost and the time spent in bed, you could hardly expect to get up and dance a jig, now could you?"

"I suppose not," Stephen said moodily. Obviously he could not expect to mount his horse and ride back to Deeford speedily either.

Thomas appeared a short time later carrying a stout cane.

"Thought you might find this of use. Father used to use it when he had an attack of the gout!"

"That's just what I feel like!" Stephen said sourly but by the time he had limped a few steps with the stick he felt better.

At his next visit Doctor Somers announced that he was entirely satisfied with Stephen's progress.

"However, do not rush things, my lord," the physician warned. "I would suggest that you wait several more days before you subject your leg to the strain of going downstairs. I shall not be calling again as I am off to London to visit my brother. Should any further treatment become necessary, my colleague, Doctor Linley, will be delighted to attend you."

"I trust that will not be necessary!" Stephen said solemnly. "But I was indeed fortunate that you were here when I needed you." He hoped the words did not sound too tongue-in-cheek.

The physician bowed. "I hope your recovery will be a speedy one, my lord," he said politely, withdrawing.

Old wind-bag, Stephen thought, lying back in his chair. What had his aunt called the man, a fusspot?

"Oh, good! You're up, Ansell! I thought I saw the physician depart." Thomas had come into the room unnoticed. "Do you think you could manage to walk across the gallery to the other wing? There is a small parlour there we have decided to use until you can get downstairs again. We have a surprise for you there!"

Stephen looked at his young cousin's slightly pink and eager face and smiled.

"In that case I'd better try, hadn't I?" he said cheerfully.

The passage in the family wing did not correspond to the one in the guest wing, as halfway along double doors led into a small parlour. Stephen guessed instantly that it was Sarah's boudoir. The green and gold furnishings were her colours. It was a lady's room but not too totally feminine. He noticed with amusement that the great green and gold tapestry which covered one wall was of a hunting scene more suited to a gentleman's apartment.

Stephen paid no more attention to the furnishings. His gaze went to the hearth, where, seated in a great chair which made her look smaller and thinner than ever, was his aunt.

"Aunt! How are you?" He limped across the room to bend over her.

She eyed him critically. "As I said once before, all the better for seeing you, Stephen! I am most happy to say

I am well on the way to being recovered — as I trust you are. But never mind about me — you have other guests, you know!"

Stephen straightened up and looked round. To his surprise he saw the room behind him was full of people. The three eldest Gleeson girls were sitting on the window-seat attended by the Comte and a young man about Thomas's age whom Stephen took to be Sir Peter Duffney's son.

Thomas grinned at Stephen. "A welcome up party!" he suggested.

9

MORRIS woke Stephen with the remark that the weather still held fair and handed him his morning mug of ale.

Stephen took the mug and grunted listlessly. If they could be on their way back to Deeford the news would be of some import, he thought, suddenly restless. Morris, sensing his master's mood, withdrew in silence and went in search of his own breakfast.

Stephen was sipping leisurely when from behind the closed dressing-closet door came the sounds of a yowl, a crash and a muffled cursing. The next instant the door was thrown open and the big grey cat shot into the room followed as far as the door by an agitated young stable-boy. For a moment he and Stephen stared at each other, the boy with a look of horror on his face, Stephen dumbfounded. The boy made as if to retreat back into the closet but Stephen recovered himself and yelled: "Come here!"

The boy came reluctantly to the bedroom side of the door.

"I . . . I beg pardon, my lord!"

"What in the name of heaven are you doing in my closet?"

"I be in the wrong room, my lord."

"I should think so! What room should you be in?"

"The Lady Sarah's."

"The Lady Sarah's? At this hour in the morning?"

"Yes, m'lord. I 'ave to find 'er maid and as I couldn't find 'er downstairs I came up to look for 'er like 'is lordship said to do."

"Lord Gerton told you to look for the maid in the Lady Sarah's bedchamber?" Stephen's black brows were raised questioningly.

The boy gave him a frightened look. "Not 'sactly, m'lord. 'Is lordship told me to find Tab and not tell anybody. If I couldn't find 'er in the kitchen I was to go up the backstairs as she'd be in the Lady Sarah's closet or bedchamber."

"Backstairs? What backstairs?"

It was the boy's turn to look puzzled. "The stairs that lead up into the dressing-closets of the end bedchambers, m'lord. But I must be in the wrong wing." He turned to make his escape back into the closet.

"Oh," Stephen murmured, glancing at the cat now settling itself on the bed beside him. So that was how it got into the room — this was not the first time it had slept on his bed. "Wait!" he said sharply to the boy. "Why did Lord Gerton send you to find Lady Sarah's maid?"

"'E said I wasn't to tell no one."

"He wouldn't have meant me!" Stephen tried to sound as convincing as he could.

"Yes, m'lord — I mean, no, m'lord!"

"Well? Why did he send you?"

The boy hesitated a moment, then blurted out: "The Lady Sarah must 'ave taken a tumble from 'er 'orse, m'lord. Star Lady returned saddled but alone to the stables a little while ago. The 'ead groom fetched Lord Gerton from 'is breakfast and 'is lordship sent me to find Tab."

"I see," Stephen said carefully. "Then

you had better find her, hadn't you! Hurry!"

"Yes, m'lord!" The boy fled thankfully.

Stephen endured the confined isolation of his bedchamber for a few minutes longer. Now that the room was silent again he could faintly hear shouts and the sound of horses. Thomas would be organising a search for his sister. Unable to bear his own inactivity any longer, he got out of bed and limping to the bell rope pulled it vigorously. Downstairs he would at least be able to find out what was going on.

Morris was horrified when he heard his master's intention.

"But, my lord, the physician said you was to wait a few days before going downstairs. Get dressed and go into the upstairs parlour if you must. I will station myself downstairs and bring you any news immediately."

"Stop your huff and bring me my clothes!"

"But you can't do anything down there, my lord!"

"I am perfectly well aware of that — nevertheless I intend to go down."

Morris, recognising the determination in his master's tone, silently fetched the clothes.

"What did you hear below stairs?" Stephen asked presently.

"Only that her ladyship went riding alone at dawn as she often does and must have been thrown. Star Lady, her ladyship's horse, was found in the stable-yard with her reins trailing." Morris did not look up.

Stephen asked no more questions but concentrated on getting dressed. Once he was ready he walked slowly and deliberately to the door.

At least I'm not so weak and stiff this morning, he thought thankfully. At the top of the stairs Morris would have taken his arm but Stephen shook him off impatiently and taking the steps one at a time he reached the bottom without undue difficulty.

He was about to seat himself on the hall settle when the passage door was thrown open and Thomas staggered into the hall with Sarah in his arms.

"Stephen!" Thomas panted in surprise. "What are you doing down here?"

"I heard Sarah had had an accident. Good God! Is she dead?"

Sarah's eyes were closed and her face was deathly white except for a scarlet streak where blood had oozed from a scratch on her cheek.

Sarah opened eyes that were too large and dark.

"The positions are reversed, are they not, cousin? Luckily I am no more dead than you were when they carried you in, in fact far less so. I am quite certain I could walk if you would put me down, Tom!"

"Not likely! I'm taking you straight up to your bed, my girl!"

Sarah, watching Stephen, said: "You shouldn't have come downstairs, cousin — For heaven's sake go and sit down before you collapse — you look as if you've seen a ghost!"

"I thought I was seeing a corpse, which is possibly worse!" Stephen replied, forcing a smile.

"Stop talking pleasantries — I can't hold you much longer!" Thomas, with one foot on the first step, shifted his grip slightly. Sarah was almost his size and no lightweight.

Sarah bit her lip, stifling a gasp of pain.

"You are hurt!" Stephen said sharply.

"She was thrown onto her back and bruised," Thomas panted as he mounted the stairs slowly. At the top he paused and called down to Stephen: "If Sir George calls keep him talking down there will you, Ansell?"

Stephen nodded, watching helplessly while Thomas carried his sister along the gallery. Then he limped slowly to the long oak settle and sank down on it. Weakness must be making him feel as he did, or more probably frustration at his own utter uselessness, he thought despondently.

He did not have long to brood. Shortly after he sat down he heard a horse coming along the driveway. The expected knock sounded and moments later he heard Burnet going to the door behind the entrance screens.

Because of Thomas's instruction Stephen had supposed that word of Sarah's accident had been sent to the Hall, so he was not in the least surprised when Sir

George entered. The lover come hot-foot to enquire after his betrothed, Stephen thought sardonically, as he rose and went to meet the man.

There was however little of the anxious lover in Sir George's manner. He was wearing an expression of highly pleased satisfaction, in fact his normally rather sour face was almost beaming. He bowed to Stephen.

"Ah! I'm pleased to see you downstairs again, Lord Ansell! And sooner than expected too. Was that wise? You don't look too strong yet — I would have taken more rest if I were you."

Again the words were polite form and Stephen answered coldly: "I am perfectly strong enough, thank you!"

"Well, you are the best judge of that, no doubt! But your weak state does give you a perfect alibi. Not that I ever seriously suspected you in any way!"

"Alibi? Suspected me of what?" Stephen asked in complete bewilderment. He had had nothing to do with Sarah falling off her horse."

Of being the Black Monk! Though of course the idea was absurd, as he started his activities long before you came to this part of the world."

"I thought the Black Monk was supposed to be a ghost!"

"Last night he was no ghost — I fought with him!"

Stephen stared curiously at Sir George. The man was almost purring with satisfaction. "I imagine you won? Did you kill the rogue?"

"No. As a matter of fact he won last night. He disarmed me and disappeared into the darkness. But no matter. Today I shall get the better of him — look!"

Sir George walked over to a table and unrolled a tightly folded bundle he had been holding under his arm. It consisted of a shirt and a black cloak with a cowl. Both the shirt and the cloak were ripped across the left shoulder and the back of the shirt was blood-soaked.

"You see! I wounded him last night. Probably not seriously but enough to mark him clearly. No man could completely hide a wound like that, so I have only to find a man with a stiff shoulder to know that he is the Black Monk!"

Stephen looked at the shirt closely. "It looks as if you stabbed the man in the back! It seems it was no fair fight?"

"My dear Lord Ansell! Who would fight fair with a man like that! In any case that occurred before we started fighting. I found the rogue about to wreck the machinery of the windmill. He had already burst down the river dyke and flooded my field. I crept up on him intending to kill him but I must have made some sound for he dodged aside."

"Sensible of him! And he got the better of you despite a hole in the shoulder! You must be out of practice, Sir George!"

Sir George flushed angrily at Stephen's jibe. "He made his escape by a trick only! Besides I do not indulge much in swordplay," he said stiffly.

"No? You were just a clerk in Cromwell's army, weren't you!" Stephen found sudden enjoyment in venting his spleen.

Sir George's flush deepened but he said with fair restraint: "A pity you were not able to fight the man, my lord! Perhaps you would have been able to finish him off there and then! However I came here to do just that! Perhaps you would be so good as to tell me where Lord Gerton is this morning? Has he risen yet from his bed?"

"Lord Gerton has been up for hours. Why?" Stephen, his mind jerked back to the present happenings of the morning, realised that Sir George did not know of Sarah's accident.

"I thought he might be lying abed nursing a sore shoulder!"

"That he is not!" Stephen informed him brusquely. "Lady Sarah had a riding accident early this morning and Lord Gerton is up with her now."

Sir George looked disconcerted. "I'm sorry. I did not know. Is she much hurt?"

"No, not seriously. I was about to send a message to you, Sir George," Thomas had come downstairs behind them unnoticed. He was in his shirt-sleeves and there was a slight wariness in his manner.

"I am relieved to hear it!" Sir George peered at Thomas. "There is blood on your shirt! If Lady Sarah is not much hurt, whose is it?"

"I said Sarah was not seriously hurt but she is slightly cut and grazed, which is where the blood comes from. A little blood goes a long way, you know!" Thomas sounded bland enough.

"Lady Sarah looked more than just grazed to me!" Stephen broke in.

Thomas shot him a look which could have been warning. "Yes, her back is extensively bruised too, Tab tells me."

"Have you sent for the physician?"

"No. We were going to but then we remembered that he had gone away. Sarah would not let me call his stand-in. She said she didn't fancy a strange man. And I really don't think she is bad enough to need a physician."

"I hope you are right!" There was a certain reluctance about Thomas that Stephen did not understand.

Thomas looked worried. "Mistress Fuller will attend her. If a day in bed doesn't help her I shall call the other physician without telling her."

"I am sure the old witch will quickly heal her, Lord Gerton!" Sir George said impatiently. "Now would you please raise your hands above your head!"

"Good Lord, why! Do you intend to shoot me? I had nothing to do with her fall." Thomas asked, puzzled.

"No. He wants to find out if you have a wounded shoulder," Stephen informed him. "Look!" He held out the blood-stained shirt.

Sir George repeated his story about the previous night while Thomas looked at him with raised brows.

"So you immediately thought I was the rogue! Sorry to disappoint you but you are quite wrong, Sir George!"

"Perhaps you would care to prove it!" Sir George asked tenaciously.

"Oh, certainly!"

Thomas fumbled with the fastenings of his shirt and the next instant he bared his unblemished shoulders. "Satisfied?"

"Quite, my lord! Thank you!" Sir George's face expressed angry disbelief.

Stephen was only slightly less surprised. He knew he should have known from the way in which Thomas had carried Sarah that he was not hurt in any way but in spite of all the denials he had been certain that Thomas had to be the Black Monk. Stephen had noticed when he picked it up that the cowl was slightly torn and had realised that it was the same one that the Black Monk had worn when he had encountered him. He had forgotten all about the threads he had twisted into his hat band and now he wondered if there were any identifying hairs with them.

Thomas pulled his shirt back over his shoulders. "Who do you suspect now, Sir George?"

"Perhaps I might have a word with Father O'Brien!" Sir George was determined to see his quest through.

"Oh, I shouldn't think that will be difficult! He is usually in the library at this time of the morning."

Thomas led the way along the passage, fastening his shirt as he went. A knock on the library door produced no reply so he opened the door and went in. The room was empty.

"Strange," Thomas said uneasily. "He usually works in here at this time. Come to think of it, I didn't see him at breakfast but then I was called away to look for Sarah almost before I had taken a mouthful. Perhaps he went to look for her after I had left and does not know that she is safely home."

"Possibly. However I should like to be certain that he is not in bed nursing his shoulder." Sir George was more sure of himself again."

No doubt I should have been told if he was," Thomas said drily. "Oh, very well! I will take you up to his bedchamber if that is the only way to convince you!"

Stephen followed them back into the hall but went to sit on the settle while Thomas conducted Sir George upstairs. They were not gone for long and returned, Thomas looking extremely worried and Sir George triumphant. Father O'Brien's bed had not been slept in the previous night.

"Where could he be?" Stephen asked, not yet ready to believe that the elderly priest could be the Black Monk.

"He rode into King's Lynn yesterday afternoon on some business or the other," Thomas replied. "He quite often meets friends there, so I thought nothing of it when he did not appear at supper. But he has never spent the night away before.

I fear some accident must have befallen him."

"Like a wound in the shoulder!"

"No, not like a stab in the back from you!" Thomas eyed his future brother-in-law with dislike. "I meant that he must have been attacked by footpads or even thrown from his horse."

Before he could speculate further Burnet appeared from the back regions and handed him a note. "A boy has just delivered it, my lord," he explained.

Thomas opened the paper and read the few lines it contained, his face losing its worried expression as he did so. He handed the note to Sir George as soon as he had finished reading.

"See the boy is rewarded and give him a meal before he leaves, Burnet." Thomas turned to Stephen. "It is from Father O'Brien," he explained rather unnecessarily. "He met an old friend who is in the district for a few days and has gone to spend the time with him. They are staying over Downham way."

"A very likely story! More like he is hiding in some inn, nursing his shoulder!"

Sir George tossed the note carelessly onto the table.

"You are doubting the word of a priest, sir!" Thomas said angrily.

"A popish priest! Since when have they been noted for telling the truth?" Sir George's voice was rising.

"A man's religion has little to do with the truth he speaks, I think!" Thomas was rapidly losing his temper and he too was almost shouting.

"Gentlemen! Not so loud, I think! The Lady Sarah is in bed to rest her hurts and here you are brawling like a pair of fighting cocks! Cousin, you should be ashamed! You'll have Lady Sarah rising from her bed to see what is going on." Stephen decided it was better to stop the wrangle before it became an open fight.

"Sorry," Thomas muttered, subsiding.

"Were she here, the Lady Sarah would undoubtedly be having her say with the rest of us!" Sir George clearly resented Stephen's intervention.

"That is beside the point," Stephen said, disgusted at the man's rudeness. "As it is, she is lying hurt and you are showing scant regard for her condition."

Sir George ignored him and turned angrily on Thomas. "Ay, and that's another thing! How is it that you allow your sister to ride out unattended, my lord? I imagine she must have been alone if you had to go out and search for her?"

"I am not my sister's keeper! She has always ridden how and when she will. Usually she takes a groom with her but perhaps this morning she thought the hour too early to call her groom from his stable duties."

"Well, when she is my wife she won't ride out how and when she wills, I can tell you that!"

"She won't thank you for it!"

"No? But then she won't be in a position to argue. As my wife she will do my bidding, not follow her will."

"What unlover-like sentiments!" Stephen jeered. "You make one wonder why you are marrying Lady Sarah when you so clearly disapprove of her!" It was dangerous ground but he was now as aroused as the other two.

Sir George retaliated instantly. "As to why, that is my business, my lord, not yours! —unless you have a desire to marry her yourself? From the way you are always rushing to her defence, anyone would think that you, not I, were betrothed to the girl!"

Stephen, suddenly white around the mouth, stared at Sir George. "Be careful! I could fight you for saying that I have behaved improperly towards your betrothed!" he said, dangerously quiet.

"Ansell! Don't be stupid!" Thomas began in alarm. He was saved from having to say anything further by the sound of footsteps in the gallery above them.

All three looked up guiltily, wondering if they could have disturbed Sarah. But it was Mr Perrington who made his way down to join them. If he noticed the strained faces and felt the tension he did not remark on it.

"Sarah does very well," he announced. "Mrs Perrington has just been in to see her and found her sleeping." He bowed to Sir George. "Good-morning, sir! I am pleased to be able to assure you that Lady Sarah is little the worse for her toss, it seems."

Sir George had the grace to express his thanks and then take his leave of them.

Mr Perrington went over to the table and picked up the torn garments. "What in the name of heaven are these?"

Thomas gave a crack of unmirthful laughter. "Sir George met with the Black Monk last night and found him flesh and blood after all! In spite of wounding the man he found himself summarily disarmed and fooled into the bargain! Naturally he is hot on the chase this morning."

"He came here to accuse you?"

"Yes. First me, then Father O'Brien!" Thomas explained about the priest's disappearance.

"So that is what you were all quarrelling about?"

"That and other things. Sir George made one accusation that was so stupid that Ansell wanted to fight him on the spot! Not that I wouldn't rather have you for a brother-in-law, cousin!" He turned to Stephen who was leaning on the high back of the settle, his colour still not returned. Thomas went on: "Somehow I don't think you'll be fighting anyone for a while. Do come and sit down, cousin. You look quite exhausted from coming downstairs and standing about."

"Your leg paining you, my boy?" Mr Perrington had also noticed Stephen's lack of colour.

He supposed it was and, nodding automatically, he sank down on the chair Thomas offered him. Sir George's stupid accusation, as Thomas termed it, was not so stupid at all — he did very much want to marry Sarah.

10

STEPHEN was sitting in the upstairs parlour with his aunt the next morning when the door opened and Sarah walked in. She was still decidedly pale and held herself stiffly but her face wore a defiant expression.

"Good morning, Aunt! Don't get up, cousin. I have merely come to join the circle of invalids!"

"Me not get up? What about you! You don't look fit enough to have left your bed!" Stephen strove to keep any excess of feeling out of his voice.

Sarah seated herself in the chair he drew up for her and cautiously leaned back against the cushions.

"I am just stiff — and who isn't after taking a toss! I found myself getting worse lying in bed."

"It must have been a mighty violent toss to make you look as you did when your brother carried you in!"

"Yes, I can't think how I didn't see

the wretched hole — I must have been daydreaming. I was lucky not to have broken any bones, I suppose."

"You were extremely foolish not to have taken your groom with you, child!" Mrs Perrington told her tartly.

"Yes, Aunt, but . . . "

"There will be no 'buts' in the future! Sarah has promised me never to ride out unattended again, so you need not scold her, Aunt!"

The door closed behind Thomas and his uncle, both dressed for riding. Stephen felt a twinge of envy.

Sarah gave her brother a look that was anything but grateful for his intervention; however she held her peace.

Thomas looked at her closely. "You should still be in bed, I think, but I am glad you have managed to rejoin us!"

"Yes, yes! Leave the girl alone! I am sure she is best able to judge the state of her well-being. I can't think what is wrong with this family — everyone is taking to his bed, one after the other!" Mr Perrington rubbed his cold hands together in front of the fire.

"You next, sir?" Thomas asked with a

grin and ignoring his uncle's snort went on: "Seriously, though, Uncle, I don't mean to be rude in suggesting that you leave my roof, but I do think that while the weather holds you should make plans to take Aunt home before the winter does fully set in. This dry weather cannot hold for much longer."

"Perhaps I could travel with you as far as London?" Stephen asked eagerly.

"Not in your present condition," Mr Perrington said firmly. "The jolting would burst open your wound — even if it didn't it would mean hours of agony. Deeford won't fall down if you don't get home for another couple of weeks, lad!"

Stephen had to acknowledge the truth of this.

The weather seemed to have held fine long enough. The sky was already dark with thickly banked clouds when Sir George arrived after dinner to see if Father O'Brien had returned. Finding his errand fruitless, he said he would not linger, excusing himself on account of the approaching storm. His horse had already been taken round to the stable-yard and Thomas followed by Sarah and Stephen conducted him out of the side door.

"I am glad I find you so well recovered, sweetheart!" Sir George remarked to Sarah, laying his arm round her shoulders.

Sarah shrank away. "I am not so feeble as to be laid up long by a toss, sir!" she said coldly, cutting off further conversation.

The whole sky had turned blue-black and seemed to be only a few feet above the roof-tops. A growl of thunder rolled across the marsh.

To break their silence Stephen asked Sarah: "You don't mind thunder, cousin?"

"No, I enjoy a good storm. But then I have never heard the roar of cannon which is supposed to be like thunder, nor have I been shipwrecked in a gale . . . " She spoke absently, her gaze on the bent figure of an old woman carrying a bucket across a corner of the yard.

Stephen, following her look, recognised old Mistress Fuller. He glanced at Sir George and was relieved to see no recognition in his face. Unfortunately, Master fuller came round the end of the building at that moment and went to take the bucket from his sister. Sir

George knew him instantly and his face darkened.

The meeting might have passed of without incident if a brilliant streak of lightning had not flashed across the clouds above the yard. Everyone was lit like actors on a stage and half bemused by the sudden brightness.

The old woman recovered first and shook her fist at Sir George. "Brand me a witch, would 'ee, thy son of Satan! See how the good God sends to strike at 'ee! 'E may miss 'ee now, but afore many moons 'ave waned 'E'll send 'ee thy just punishment. Remember this — when fire and air and water strike at 'ee, 'ee shall know thy hour 'as come. 'Ee called me a child of Satan, but the good God will send 'ee down into the fire forever — and all the rains of 'eaven cant quench that!"

Abruptly the old woman took her brother's arm to lead him away. His face frozen with fear, Master Fuller allowed himself to be led round the corner of the stables.

In the yard no one moved until a sudden flurry of rain-drops broke the spell. Sir George, visibly pale, seized his horse and, ignoring the threatening deluge, rode out of the yard without a word. The Perringtons and Stephen, also wordless, moved hurriedly towards the house, leaving the stable-hands to calm the nervous animals.

At supper that night Thomas was preoccupied and disinclined to discuss the incident but not so Mrs Perrington, who had heard the story from her maid.

"I hear our resident witch has been accursing Sir George!" she remarked cheerfully, looking round the table.

"Yes," Thomas said reluctantly. "There can't be any truth or power in it, but it certainly was eerie the way she said it with the lightning flashing and the thunder rolling round."

"She was not cursing him, she was foretelling his future, and Sir George half believes her!" Sarah said scornfully.

"Wouldn't you worry if your doom was foretold in such a manner?" Stephen asked.

"Not if it were foretold by Mistress Fuller!" Sarah had no cause to believe in the old woman's prophecies. "I thought we were agreed that she is just a harmless old woman and no witch."

"No witch perhaps, but I'm not so sure about her being harmless," he said thoughtfully.

Before brother and sister could ask him what he meant Mrs Perrington enquired: "What exactly did the old woman tell Fanworth? That he is about to die?"

"Not exactly. She said he was going to be attacked by fire, water and wind and go down into hellfire forever, I think." Thomas wrinkled up his brow in an attempt to remember.

"I should think the hellfire is a foregone conclusion!" Stephen said under his breath.

Thomas heard him and repressed a grin. Mrs Perrington was saying: "A vague kind of prediction! But awkward for you if the old woman is going to go about cursing all your guests, Gerton!"

"I'll speak to her in the morning," Thomas said uneasily and turned the topic of conversation to Father O'Brien's absence. However for the rest of the meal he was partly preoccupied and as they left the dining-parlour he drew his uncle quietly away to the library where they remained closeted together most of the evening.

The storm blew over in the night, with surprisingly little rain falling. The next morning the sun dominated the few scudding clouds that were still about. Looking down from a window of the upstairs parlour about mid morning, Stephen saw Thomas and Mr Perrington riding off, both dressed in their best riding clothes. Stephen smiled to himself — he had a pretty fair idea of where they were bound and later said as much to Sarah when he met her on his way to the stables. He had not seen his horse since the night of the shooting.

"I see Gerton and our uncle have gone out visiting this morning. I imagine they have gone to pay a call on Mr Gleeson?"

"Oh, so you have guessed! Poor Tom hardly slept last night, torn between the prospect of delight and horror at the thought of the interview! Left to himself, Tom would have put it off, I think, but it had to be now while Uncle is here to speak for him and settle the details of the contract." Sarah fell into step beside him.

"I wish him joy." Stephen said sincerely.

"So do I." Then a shade too quickly: "Where are you going? Not riding surely?"

"No," he said striving to keep the frustration out of his voice. "I will obey the good Doctor Somers orders a little longer! I thought I would take a look at the horses, that's all."

Sarah glanced up at him. "How you must hate being cooped up here when you have so much to do at home," she said with quiet sympathy.

He did not deny it but said with as much gallantry as he could muster: "There are far worse places to be cooped up in than Banks House, I can assure you!"

Sarah shrugged. "Any place is prison if you have the desire to be away from it." Then abruptly changing the subject: "It is a pity you could not have gone to call on Mr Gleeson with Tom and Uncle this morning. I am sure Mr Gleeson would favour your suit with Lucy, and Uncle will be gone in a few days."

"You are as bad as Aunt Bess — trying to marry me off at every opportunity!"

Stephen had spent most of his waking hours the last day or two mulling over in his mind the Question of whether he should ask Lucy to be his wife. Apart from being well endowed she was gentle, kind and understanding, also intelligent — a rare combination of qualities, he readily acknowledged, and marriages had been founded on far less, he knew. He accepted that he could never marry Sarah but could he ever get her out of his heart and his mind? What if Lucy should fall in love with him? Being in the throes of his first deep consuming passion himself, it did not seem fair to take her love and her life and to have nothing to give in return. For her it would be a good marriage from the social point of view but from what he had already learned of Lucy's nature she would care little for that. He remembered Richard Moxton's jibe. A title could be a hollow thing when dreams withered away.

Aware that Sarah was looking at him, he said: "I am old enough to speak for myself, you know! Besides I thought you told me to keep out of your affairs — now you are meddling in mine."

"Touché!" Sarah admitted, opening the half door which led into the horse stalls.

The big horse raised his head when he saw his master and came to nuzzle his shoulder. Stephen leant his cane against the partition wall and pulled the horse's mane affectionately. Looking over at Sarah who had followed him inside he asked: "Star Lady was not hurt when she stepped into the hole?"

"Hole?"

"Why, yes — when she threw you."

"Oh! . . . no, luckily she came to no harm at all. Davis could find nothing wrong with her, thank goodness."

"So the misfortune was all yours!"

"Fortunately, yes — I shall mend far sooner than she would have if she had hurt a leg."

"That is one way to look at it, to be sure!" he said, amused.

"Oh, come now! Wouldn't you rather have that hole in your leg than a dead horse?"

"Put it that way, I suppose I

would — now that it is healed up, anyway! But you were lucky not to break your back as Uncle did."

"My blessings are many!" she said derisively, turning away.

Stephen looked at her as she leaned over Star Lady's stall. In the dimness her hair gleamed with a soft burnished light, the bunches of curls falling forward to hide her face. For a moment he was reminded of the innkeeper's daughter as she had bent over to draw his ale. The feeling she had aroused in him had been pure sexual appetite, which had blazed, been fed and died so completely that now he had to think carefully to remember her name. Sarah filled him with longing too but also with so much more. Uppermost was the desire to protect her and to see her really happy. There was a dejected droop to her shoulders which her hair did not hide. It was tied high as usual but there was an escaped tendril curling in the nap of her neck which he longed desperately to reach out and touch.

Tearing his eyes away from her, he gave Land-Lubber a final pat and picked up his cane.

Outside the sunlight seemed very bright and for a moment neither Stephen nor Sarah saw Mistress Fuller walking towards them. Stephen, intent on watching Sarah as she latched the door behind them, started when a voice bid him good-day.

Sarah, recognising the voice, turned round quickly. "Ah, Mistress Fuller! You caused quite a stir yesterday! My brother is most upset that you cursed one of his guests. Surely it is no manner in which to repay him for giving you shelter?"

"It weren't no curse, my lady. I was just warning him of what be coming to him!" the old woman muttered, her eyes downcast.

"I believe you, but it would be much the wisest if you did not do so," Sarah said in a kinder tone. "If you go round telling tales like that people will say you are indeed a witch!"

"I b'aint no witch! But I look about me and I see things. Some o' the things belong to the future, but a gift o' the sight don't mean I be a witch!"

"True. But many innocent people have been burned at the stake for less."

"I know that, my lady, and I be

grateful for his lordship and you saving me."

"Lord Ansell helped too."

"For which I give 'ee hope." The old woman looked directly at him.

He did not understand her. "You have already healed my leg — for which I give you my most heartfelt thanks, mistress!"

She continued to stare fixedly at him. "I said I give 'ee hope," she said as if she had not heard him. "The time of despair will pass and your love will have its chance." Her glance flicked to Sarah, then back to Stephen. "The way to happiness will not be easy, but eventually 'ee'll go from here and forget the evil of the marshes and the raging of the sea. To 'ee the seventh wave be friend not foe. Contentment shall come to 'ee both."

"Now I know you are crazy," Sarah began, then stopped.

Beside her Stephen was standing very still, leaning on his cane. Beneath his faded tan his face had gone a dull red and his eyes were full of bitter rage as he stared at the old woman.

For a long moment there was silence

between them and only the sound of horses came from the stalls. Sarah looked up at Stephen and comprehension filled her eyes. "Oh, Stephen, I am so sorry," she said softly.

"You are sorry!" he said savagely. "I had intended to spare you this and now the interfering old witch . . . " he turned to vent his anger on the old woman but Mistress Fuller had slipped away into one of the buildings, leaving them alone.

Not for long. The sound of hooves coming nearer heralded the return of one of the stable-hands with some of his charges. With one accord Stephen and Sarah walked out of the yard and into the garden.

"I am so sorry," Sarah repeated. "Your coming here has brought you more ill than comfort, I think."

"The latest ill, as you call it, is purely my own fault. I knew before I came here that you were betrothed."

"You knew?"

"Yes. A gossiping friend in London told me. And if I did not wish to believe him Aunt took good care to inform me of the fact as soon as I arrived."

"No doubt they told you I have little dowry too!"

"They did though both could have saved their breath!"

In an attempt to divert him she asked: "What did Mistress Fuller mean about the seventh wave?"

"It is an old seaman's superstition — when times are bad it is the seventh wave that brings disaster," he said briefly. That part of the prediction did not interest him.

Sarah thought back to their earlier conversation. "And I have been teasing you to offer for Lucy."

"Now you see my dilemma!" he said sardonically. "I have the highest regard for Mistress Lucy — she is one of the nicest young ladies I have ever met. So it does not seem right to ask her to be my wife when I have no love to give her in exchange."

"You think that now but you will come to forget me in time. Memories do fade, you know, Stephen."

"Like your love for Master Carr?" he asked bitterly.

Sarah winced but said quietly: "John is dead and so must I be . . . for you."

"Forgive me. I should not have said that," he said quickly.

In the trees the birds chirped and from the marsh came the harsh cries of the gulls but in the garden the silence grew. Sarah's face became mask-like but her eyes were filled with anguish and to hide their expression she bent and plucked a daisy which she twisted and crushed until it was a mess of pulp.

Stephen broke the silence. "You once told me that you would never break the promise you made to your father just for the love of another man, so I would not ask you to break it for a man you do not love. You need not worry that I will speak of this again. Believe me, I would have given much to have saved you from this embarrassment. I shall leave Banks House at the first possible moment." His voice was very low.

Sarah dropped the mangled daisy and for a moment she raised her eyes, dark amber, to his face. "Stephen." Her voice was as low as his. “I would rather have known than not known.”

Swiftly she walked away, leaving him to punch holes savagely with his cane in the newly scythed turf.

11

THOMAS and his uncle returned in the late afternoon, having stayed to dine with the Gleesons. Thomas was patently full of his own happiness and Mr Perrington showed obvious relief that his part in the affair was over and the contract terms agreed to.

Sarah hugged her brother. “How happy I am for you, Tom!” she said sincerely.

Stephen echoed her words as he shook his young cousin’s hand. “When is the happy day to be?” he enquired, stifling a pang of envy.

“Oh, not till early next June, when I am out of mourning,” Thomas replied, beaming happily. “Pity you could not ride with us, Ansell, for I’m sure Mr Gleeson would be happy to welcome you as a second son-in-law! He really is quite approachable, you know, and not at all difficult to talk to.”

“I met Mr Gleeson while you were still

in the school-room!" Stephen told him crushingly but with a half-smile.

"Oh, yes, while you were on one of your secret missions, I suppose. Well, if he knows you he would find your suit doubly welcome, I'm sure."

"Actually he knows little enough about me — in those days the less one knew about anyone else the better!"

"But didn't I see you talking to him on the night of the party?"

"You did — we drank the King's health, so that does not mean I have entered the matrimonial stakes!"

"Well, why don't you? You seem to get on well enough with Mistress Lucy — why, the first thing she said today was how were you?"

"The devil she did!" Stephen turned away to hide his confusion.

"Give over, Tom, do!" Sarah said swiftly. "You know our cousin has to put his estate in order before he can look for a bride."

"The thing is," Thomas said carefully. "If he has a mind for Mistress Lucy he had better not leave it too long to ask permission to court her, or he might find he has competition!"

"What do you mean?"

"Francis Duffney and de Verais arrived shortly before Uncle and I departed. De Verais had eyes for no one but Mistress Lucy and, in spite of him being a Frenchman, Mr Gleeson did not seem adverse to the situation!"

Stephen's startled gaze met Sarah's, then, before either of them could comment, there was a commotion in the side passage leading to the stables and Father O'Brien walked into the hall.

He looked perfectly fit and most unlike a man who had been lying up waiting for a wound to heal. Aware of several pairs of speculative eyes watching him, his expression became a trifle defensive.

Turning to Thomas when the first greetings were over, he asked abruptly; "I trust I did not inconvenience you in any way by not returning the other night, Thomas? The meeting with my old friend was totally unexpected but turned out to be extremely propitious! I have found a position for myself which I can take up almost immediately." His usually severe face became lit with a smile.

"But that is wonderful news, Father!" Thomas beamed back. Then he hastily added: "Though you know there will always be a home for you with us, wherever we may be."

"Thank you, Thomas," Father O'Brien said with twitching lips. "However I greatly prefer to follow the active occupation of my calling."

"What are you going to do, Father?" Sarah asked.

"My friend has secured for me the position of tutor and private chaplain to a Mr Howard, who is, I believe, a very distant relation of the Earl of Suffolk."

Stephen, who had often wondered if Father O'Brien's habitual glum and censorious outlook stemmed from his feeling of utter uselessness in his present position, said sincerely: "Congratulations, Father! Long may the King keep his present liberal views!"

"Amen!" Father O'Brien said fervently. Then turning back to Thomas he repeated: "As I was saying, I hope I did not cause any inconvenience by not returning the other night?"

"Lord, no! You did not put us out

in any way but your disappearance has caused you to become the prime suspect in Fanworth's latest brush with the Black Monk!" Thomas said cheerfully.

Father O'Brien listened in astonishment while Thomas went on to explain how Sir George had first stabbed and then fought with the Black Monk. "Of course his first suspect was me, but unfortunately for him he was speedily forced to acquit me! So your sudden disappearance was a godsend, you must admit. A more highly suspicious circumstance could hardly be credited!"

"Well, Sir George may just as speedily acquit me — I am quite able to prove my innocence!" Father O'Brien said grimly, wriggling his shoulders. "He will find no incriminating scars on my back!"

Stephen, watching the priest's movements, had his thoughts on the strands which might still be twisted into his hatband. And now was the time to look, he decided, making his way up to his bed chamber. The hat he had worn on the ill-fated night was on a shelf in the dressing-closet. It had been neatly cleaned but the threads and hairs, unnoticed by Morris, were still twisted into the band. He pulled them free and went back into the bedchamber.

In the brightness of the big room three hairs glowed like burnished copper. If he had not known Thomas was definitely not the Black Monk Stephen would have sworn that the hairs came from Thomas's head; as it was, they had to have belonged to Father O'Brien. The priest's hair was heavily streaked with white, so Stephen supposed he must have grabbed a red tuft. It was just possible that the wound the man had received had been little more than a scratch that had healed in the few days. Father O'Brien could be hoping to bluff his way out, banking on Sir George's respect for his calling, though Sir George showed scant respect for anyone.

The whole thing just did not make sense. What had prompted the priest to take up what amounted to criminal activities — boredom? Any of the villagers must surely have a far greater grudge against Sir George than the Perrington family and it was quite possible that one or more of the village men had red hair. But who among them was educated sufficiently to have the art of swordplay or to speak French? John Carr might have been but he was dead; his father, the Perrington's steward, was dark-haired, turning grey.

* * *

Although the warmth of the summer had gone the weather remained dry and two days later Mr and Mrs Perrington were ready to start on their journey south. A rather tearful Mrs Perrington was assisted into the coach and well wrapped in rugs, while she continued to protest that she wanted to see her only niece married.

Sarah hugged her. "Hush, Aunt! My wedding-day will be the happier for knowing that you are safely home in a so much less bleak part of the country. Perhaps Sir George will bring me on a visit to you some day," she added.

Mrs Perrington smiled through her tears. Both knew this was highly unlikely but it was a thought to hold on to.

Mr Perrington gripped Stephen's hand. "Send me word as soon as you are on your way home and I'll see the gold reaches you without delay," he promised.

"Thank you, Uncle," Stephen said simply as he handed the old gentleman up into the coach.

The departure of his aunt and uncle left Stephen feeling more restless than ever. Resolved to be on his way home as soon as possible, he went upstairs and rang for Morris to bring his riding clothes.

"I'm only going to walk up the lane, you fool!" he snapped when Morris dared to protest.

The ride was not quite the success that Stephen had hoped it would be. Twisting into the saddle from the mounting block caused him the worst stab of pain he had experienced since first getting out of bed after the shooting and he was forced to admit to himself that he was not yet healed enough to mount from ground level. Walking the horse he could manage without trouble but even a few yards of slow trot brought on a throbbing ache in the bone where the ball had smashed into it. Clearly he was not going to be able to travel any distance at all for the time being. He returned to the house somewhat white-faced, but determined to ride each day until he was able to cover a reasonable distance.

He found his cousins in the hall as he was on his way to change. Sarah, noting his riding suit and worsened limp, said nothing but Thomas, misinterpreting Stephen's eagerness to be in the saddle again, said impulsively: "Do take the coach if you want to go visiting, cousin! It would never do to let de Verais get a lead over you!"

Stephen declined with a smile which he hoped was not too forced and continued on his way upstairs.

Morris took one look at his master's set face and drew his own conclusion. Deciding that divertion was the best cure, he launched into a grisly tale he had heard in the servants hall about how exceptionally high tides in the Ouse Estuary had once washed away the ground boardering a cemetery, leaving exposed bodies which were washed right out of their graves by the next high tides.

Stephen wrinkled his nose in disgust, his mind only half on the story. However he remembered it later that afternoon when he was helping his cousins entertain visitors.

Lucy and Anne, escorted by the Comte, had ridden over to bid farewell to Mr and Mrs Perrington.

"Oh, I am so sorry we have missed them!" Anne said contritely. "Mr Perrington said that they would be leaving for home soon but we did not realise it would be this soon."

"It was rather a rush," Sarah explained. "We decided it would be better for them to go while the weather remained dry and Aunt well enough to travel. A winter here would be sure to kill her — the physician said as much."

"How you will miss them!" Anne said warmly. "But then you will soon be married and going away yourself, won't you Lady Sarah?"

"Quite soon, yes," Sarah said with brittle brightness.

Anne turned to Stephen. "What a pity you have not been able to see much of our neighbourhood, my lord — There are some interesting places round about here — "

"Like a graveyard where the bodies are washed away by the high tide?" he teased her, remembering Morris's story.

"Oh, you have heard that tale, have you? The cemetery is on the other side of the estuary in Old Lynn. It happened some years ago when the river changed course after a flood. At the time I thought it was gloriously gruesome and I had nightmares about it for ages after I heard the story!" Anne laughed.

"I am not surprised, mademoiselle — it is not a story for a young lady, surely?" De Verais sounded prim but his eyes were laughing.

"What about the grave of Hickofrix in Tilney churchyard? The gravestone is nearly eight feet long! It is said that Hickofrix slew a giant by using a cartwheel as a shield and a tree as a weapon." Sarah, more talkative than usual, was not to be outdone by Anne.

"I think the story has got mixed up over the years and it was the giant who used the cartwheel and who lies buried in the churchyard," Thomas remarked.

"But the grave does exist to that size, for I have seen it myself!"

The thought came to Stephen that it had been someone's intention that he should lie beneath a tombstone in a local churchyard. Aloud he said: "Frankly, I would much prefer to see the Priory ruins — I might even see the Prior's ghost!"

"I doubt it! And the walking is very rough there," Sarah said immediately.

Speaking at the same time, Lucy said equally impulsively: "Oh, don't go there! The Black Monk might have another shot at you!"

"Don't worry, I'm not going anywhere very far at the moment," Stephen soothed. Suddenly he realised that those words were almost the first Lucy had spoken that afternoon. She had been strangely reserved all through the visit — she and Sarah might have exchanged personalities for the afternoon. He wondered fleetingly if she were ill but she looked well enough, only tense. Surely de Verais had not upset her? The Comte, laughing now with Sarah and Anne, flirted with all the girls, it seemed, but he was too much of a gentleman to make himself objectionable.

Unaware of Stephen's scrutiny, de Verais remarked reluctantly: "Unless we set out for your home immediately, ladies, we shall be riding in the dark!"

In the days that followed Stephen took to wandering slowly about the sea marsh on horseback. The marsh lay behind the great mound of clay and peat which formed the Sea Wall. This had formed a buffer against the sea since Roman times but was now much eroded. There was little stone in the area to strengthen it and the sea broke through with increasing frequency. The desolation and empty bleakness fitted in with his mood. The plaintive cries of the birds and the wind forever sighing in the reeds became a part of his depression. But there was a sense of freedom in the place too. The streams meandered at will, not bound by the normal routine of heading straight for the sea, and God alone knew where the birds went when they rose above the marsh and swooped off into the sky, leaving their wild cries to drift on the wind.

Stephen could understand why Sarah

used to ride over the marsh so often. These days there was no sign of her. He wondered if she were deliberately avoiding him, though he preferred to think she was busy with the preparations for her wedding, which could well be true, he thought.

Darkness came noticeably earlier each afternoon and once Stephen almost found himself fog-bound. It had been a still, dark day. With no wind to chill him, and his strength much improved, he had ridden further than usual. The mist crept silently in from the sea to join the wisps which began to rise above the pools and sluggish streams. With the mist came an almost tangible feeling of evil. Stephen, coming across a scum-covered pool much like the one his cousin had dragged old Mistress Fuller out of, felt it would not be hard to believe in ghosts and witchcraft in such a place. Wrapping his cloak firmly round him, he urged Land-Lubber towards higher ground and Banks House.

Sarah met him in the hall. In the firelight she looked pale and out of temper.

"You are asking for trouble riding alone in the mist," she told him sharply. "Someone has a grudge against you, real or imaginary, and just because they didn't manage to kill you last time doesn't mean they won't try again."

"I'm sorry." He could see she was genuinely worried. "It came along so suddenly. But, as you can see, no harm has befallen me!"

"Fortunately for you!" Sarah flounced away towards the kitchen quarters.

12

AFTER several days of bad weather conditions began to improve. The steady rain turned into showers and there were brief moments of sunshine, though the wind, if anything, was stronger. It was still no weather to venture far in but Thomas hailed it as a sign of better conditions to come.

"It'll be fine and calmer tomorrow," he said optimistically. "You'll be able to go out, I'm sure."

Stephen lacked his optimism but on this occasion Thomas proved to be correct. During the night the gale died away to infrequent gusts and although there were still wild ribbons of cloud in the sky there was little likelihood of rain. Stephen donned his riding clothes with relief. Another day spent boxed up inside the house would have sent him climbing the walls, he felt sure.

Land-Lubber was frisky and Stephen had difficulty in holding him back.

However he was greatly cheered to find that a brisk canter along the lane produced no ill effects. Any day now I can start for home, he thought, and felt lighter-hearted than he had for weeks.

Stephen was curious to see the sluice gates he had heard his cousins talking about. Sarah said they should be closed to prevent a combination of wind and high tides, which might occur at any time, from flooding the sea marsh. Sir George apparently had decreed that the gates remain open so that the river should not flood. As the gates were on his land, there was little the Perringtons could do about the situation. Stephen turned out of the lane and headed for the Sea Wall. Everywhere the pools were much bigger and the marsh at the foot of the wall was now under water, he noticed.

Presently he came within sight of the structure he guessed to be the gates. Squinting into a sudden burst of sunlight, Stephen realised he was not the first to visit the gates that morning. Sarah was standing on the raised river bank, holding her horse, and as Stephen watched he saw Sir George ride up and lean down to speak to her. Abruptly Stephen reined in. He had no wish to intrude in what Sarah would surely term was none of his business. He did not doubt that Sarah and Sir George would be arguing about the gates and he had no knowledge to support whether the gates should be open or closed at this time of the year.

Stephen was about to ride back the way he had come when a movement by one of the distant figures froze him in the saddle. Sir George had raised his riding crop and lashed at Sarah. Sarah's cry of mingled shock and pain reached Stephen as only a faint sigh in the wind, hardly distinguishable from the cries of the gulls, but it was enough to bring him back to life. He was riding without spurs but a violent kick sent his surprised horse bounding forward. Almost before Sir George could raise the crop a second time Stephen had closed the distance between them. Sarah saw him coming but Sir George, shouting abuse at her, was left in a state of open-mouthed amazement when Stephen urged his horse up onto the bank and snatched the crop from his hand.

As he pulled his horse up and round Stephen sent the crop flying over the width of the Sea Wall and out into the boiling sea. "You blackguard!" he snarled at Sir George. "You great bully! Here, try some of your own punishment" His sword was out by now and he hit Sir George a resounding blow with the flat of it.

All the rage seething within him went into Stephen's blow and Sir George, fumbling for his sword and still recovering from the surprise of Stephen's sudden appearance on the scene, offered scant resistance. Too late one of his hands grabbed at the pommel of his saddle. The next moment he toppled unceremoniously from the saddle and thudded onto the ground. The impacted clay of the bank was harder than it looked and he lay in an unmoving heap.

Stephen kicked his feet free of the stirrups and swung himself down to the ground. Sarah had not moved. She was still standing with one hand holding her riding skirt out of the mud and the other holding Star Lady's reins. Tossing his own reins over the patient Land-Lubber's neck, Stephen went swiftly to her side and, taking the reins from her unresisting hand, caught her to him. The moment he touched her the stiffness went out of her and she leaned against him, her face buried in his shoulder, while her breath came and went in jerking sobs.

Looking down at her he could see the bright red weal left by the lash across the back of her neck. Stephen slowly lifted his hand and very gently began to stroke a wisp of her hair. He was trembling too now and it was not just from anger, he well knew.

His touch pulled Sarah together and she twisted away from him like a startled animal. She bent to pick up her hat which had fallen off when Sir George had struck her. When she faced Stephen again she was fully in control of her expression; only her quick breathing and the darkened amber of her eyes betrayed her agitation. Deliberately she went over to where Sir George was lying and knelt beside him.

Looking up at Stephen she said quietly: "Thank you, cousin, but you should not have done it. Not hit him like that, I mean."

"Not hit him? I should have killed him! Good God, must I stand meekly by and let that great oaf bully you! Any gentleman — any man — would have hit him and I love you."

Sarah glanced half fearfully at the man on the ground but he was still unconscious and would hear nothing. Slowly she began to straighten his limbs, then choosing her words carefully, she said: "I know that. But you have only made things worse. I know that between gentlemen to hit with the flat of the sword is a grievous insult. As soon as he regains consciousness there will be trouble — that is, if he is not dead!"

Stephen hitched Star Lady and Sir George's horse to the sluice gate structure and came to kneel unwillingly on the other side of the still form. Expertly he ran his hands over Sir George's limbs.

"No, he's not dead. No bones broken even, more's the pity!" He folded Sir George's cloak into a wad and pushed it under his head. "I would say he will be coming round before long and I think you should be away before he does. Can you ride?"

"Oh, yes." Sarah's hand went unconsciously to her shoulder. When she took it away her fingers were tipped with blood. She would have wiped them quickly on her dress but Stephen had seen.

"The swine! How could he hit you so hard as to bring blood!"

"The tip must have caught me," Sarah murmured, wrapping her cloak round herself, as if to prevent him from touching her. "Forget it. Please."

"Forget it! How can I just turn my back and forget it? How can I stand by and watch you marry a brute like that?" Stephen's voice was harsh with the force of his feelings. He had promised her once that he would never mention his love for her again but he had to make the appeal or ever be less than a man in his own sight.

Sarah sensed what was passing through his mind and steeled herself against him.

"Cousin, I once told you that nothing, not love, not anyone, would make me break the promise I made to my father. Please don't make it more difficult for me to keep my vow."

"So you admit it is difficult for you to keep it now! Things have changed, have they not?"

"Vows are rarely easy to keep. Things have changed, yes, but not my purpose. It is chiefly you who have changed, cousin.

In a way this was the truth. He tried a different tack.

"Is your brother worthy of the ruin of your life?"

At the mention of Thomas Sarah's face softened and an almost maternal look stole over it. "Yes, I think so. There is an uncomplicated goodness in Tom and he deserves more than Father left him. Besides he is my little brother . . . "

"And all your life you have protected and given him everything," he finished for her, striving to keep the bitterness out of his tone. "In repayment he lets you wed a monster."

She faced him steadily. "Tom would protect me to the ends of the earth and you know it. That is why he must know nothing of my reasons." Sarah glanced down at the man lying between them.

"Long before you came, cousin, I had everything worked out to my way very satisfactorily. Please let it remain like that. It is true that the situation has changed slightly and my life means more to me now, but I still intend to keep my word.

Stephen was on his feet now and he looked down at her, his eyes suddenly narrowing as the perfect solution presented itself to him.

"Sarah!" he said through clenched teeth. "Do you mean to commit suicide?"

She looked at him, startled, but her answer came almost without hesitation. "No, I do not! I have no desire to burn in the everlasting fires of Hell, you may rest assured of that, even if it would be the easiest way out!" She got slowly to her feet, dusting down her skirt. "Besides, if I were to kill myself, how would it avenge John's death?"

John. Stephen had forgotten him in the current tussle. Perhaps he would get to the heart of the affair at last.

"How can you avenge an accident? You told me John died during a riot."

"True — he did, but not from a stray

bullet. He was deliberately shot."

"You mean he was murdered? By whom?"

Again Sarah's glance flicked to the man lying at their feet.

"Sir George had John killed." Her voice was toneless as she turned and walked towards her horse.

Stephen stared. "Fanworth! Are you sure?"

"Quite certain, though I have no proof. Just as I am certain that it was he who had you shot."

"But why, in heaven's name? To the best of my knowledge, I have never harmed more than his pride."

"Neither did John, wittingly. But John was a threat to Sir George marrying me. And for that same reason he is afraid of you — hence he attempted to have you killed. If I had shown more partiality for the Comte de Verais no doubt there would have been an attempt to remove him too. Sir George is more than fanatical about his dreams, you know. Draining his lands has come to be an obsession that fills his whole life."

Stephen digested this. "If what you say

is true we should go to the constable. Murder is not for private individuals to avenge."

"I told you — I have no proof."

The whole thing sounded like madness to Stephen. He said gently: "You would do much better to marry de Verais and go right away with him. He once said you were the most beautiful girl he had ever set eyes on. Would you marry him if he asked you?"

"You are forever trying to get me married and sent away, cousin!" She mocked him, but without sting.

"You haven't answered my question."

Sarah raised her brows. "He has never asked me."

"I know. But he is too much of a gentleman to embarrass a betrothed lady. However he also once said that all is fair in love and war. If you were to break off your betrothal I am sure he . . . "

"You know I cannot — I will not — do that!"

"You could if you wanted to. You say that Banks House is your dowry. You could sell it to Sir George — he will get it either way and something might be contrived with the money for your brother."

"Then I should be totally without a dowry and I don't think the Comte would be that noble! But as I don't intend to marry him he won't be put to the test!"

If I could marry you I wouldn't quibble about a dowry, Stephen thought, but kept the thought to himself.

"Just what do you intend to do, Sarah?" he asked.

"Take my revenge for everything."

"That tells me nothing."

"Then nothing will have to suffice you!"

Speaking slowly, he said: "I once promised you that I would not meddle in matters which do not concern me, but now this whole thing is very much my concern. Revenge, if any is to be taken, is my affair too now. So will you please tell me what you mean to do?"

"No, I will not!" Sarah unhitched Star Lady and when she turned back to Stephen there were faint spots of colour in her pale cheeks. "Go home, Stephen. Please. Just leave me alone to do what I have to."

"Alone out here with him when he comes round?"

"No. You know perfectly well what I mean — return to your own home at Deeford. You have been wanting to go for long enough!"

He assisted her into the saddle, then looked up at her, his expression as determined as her own. "Nothing is going to make me leave before your wedding-day now."

"You will only become involved in more trouble if you stay," she warned him.

"I can watch out for myself!"

"Can you? But perhaps you will be happier if you know that everything is completely settled." She looked away across the marsh as she spoke and the wind almost snatched the words from her lips.

After a glance at Sir George Stephen took Land-Lubber by the bridle and walked to where a projecting ledge of mortar on the sluice structure would serve as a mounting-block. Once astride, he came back to her.

"Nothing is ever completely settled until one is dead!" he told her grimly.

Sarah stared at him, startled, but she made no reply. A shred of cloud blotted out the sun and in an instant the expanse of water and marsh became grey and menacing. On the ground Sir George stirred slightly and moaned.

Sarah shivered. "We must hurry. We have left him lying unaided for far too long. Perhaps you would ride into the village and fetch help for him?"

"Certainly," Stephen replied formally.

They rode across the marsh in silence but when they reached the lane where Stephen must leave her to ride into the village Sarah drew rein.

"Stephen?" she spoke almost timidly. "Please don't mention any of this to Tom, will you?"

"How am I to explain to your brother that I knocked Sir George from his horse and have insulted him? Sir George is fully entitled to ask for satisfaction." Stephen spoke wearily. He could foresee endless complications from his hasty action.

"Couldn't you just leave it and see what Sir George does. He may not be in a fit state to do anything for a few days."

"I scarcely think a broken head will render Sir George harmless for long! But it shall be as you wish." He bowed low in the saddle and rode away towards the village.

13

IN the solitude of his bedchamber late that night Stephen reached for his pipe and tobacco. For a few minutes filling the pipe and lighting it with a taper from the fire occupied him. Then he seated himself by the fire and sat smoking in short, jerky puffs while his thoughts chased round in his mind. He had told Thomas that he had come across Sir George lying on the river bank with his horse near by. Alone, there was nothing he could do for Sir George, so he had gone to the village for help. Sir George would give the lie to his story soon enough but that was the least of Stephen's worries.

Sarah could not be allowed to marry a sadistic madman. Stephen's whole being revolted at the thought but how was he to stop her? She was set on the marriage as if her life depended on it. Nothing he said ever seemed to move her one iota. Only one thing could explain her determination — Sir George must have some hold over her, and a strong one at that. If only he could gain her confidence he might find some means to break that hold.

Suddenly Stephen almost laughed. An easier solution had come to him and it was really very simple. Sir George, if he were any man at all, would demand restitution for the insult of being hit by the flat of a sword. He, Stephen, would be honour bound to accept the challenge and during the duel he would have to kill Sir George. It was as simple as that. The idea of deliberately setting out to kill a man in cold blood appalled him but if what Sarah said was true Sir George would not hesitate to kill him. It was the perfect answer to the problem but he realised that the results would not be so simple. There would be a great scandal and for different reasons his cousins would probably never forgive him. However Sarah's freedom would be worth the risk.

His pipe was out now and he had decided on bed when he thought he heard soft footsteps in the passage outside his door. Seizing his sword, he tiptoed to the door and flung it open.

The passage outside was empty. The light shaft from his room lit as far as the end of the passage beyond his dressing-closet and in the other direction perhaps half the way to the gallery. For a full minute Stephen stood in the doorway peering up and down the passage but there was nothing to be seen or heard. After a last look he closed the door and carefully bolted it. The closet door had no bolt but at least it left danger from one direction only.

Thoughtfully he took a candle and went to hunt in the closet for his travelling pistol. This he primed and placed on a small stool next to his bed. Previously Stephen had ignored Sarah's fears for his safety but now he was more ready to believe her. The footfalls he had just heard were not his imagination, of that he was certain. It was a long time before he slept that night.

He was awakened next morning at the usual time by Morris opening the window curtains. If Morris saw anything strange in his master's bolting himself into his bedchamber and sleeping with a pistol at his side he said nothing. Stephen did not enlighten him.

As he dressed Stephen was apprehensive. The solution he had decided on last night was too easy — easy solutions had a habit of going wrong, he knew. With the grace of God the duel would have the necessary outcome. He did not count himself a top swordsman, especially with his weak leg, but he did not think that Sir George was an expert either.

The first sign that things were not going according to plan occurred during the morning when no communication came from Sir George. Stephen had expected to have Sir George's demand early that day and he felt let down when no word came. He cheered himself up with the thought that perhaps Sir George was too ill to worry about satisfaction at the moment but that seemed completely out of character with the man's choleric disposition.

Shortly before noon Thomas sent a man to find out how his future brother-in-law was doing. The message came back after dinner that Sir George was recovering well. Stephen received this news with mixed feelings. If Sir George was not seriously hurt, why had he not issued his challenge?

Early in the afternoon Thomas announced he was going to ride over to visit Anne. He invited Stephen to accompany him but Stephen, feeling honour bound to stay near the house in case Sir George made a move, declined. Thomas did not press him and rode cheerfully away to see his beloved. When he returned he bore tidings which were not wholly welcome.

Stephen was standing looking moodily into the hall fire and Sarah was on her way downstairs when the side door crashed open and Thomas came stamping along the passage, his face bearing an expression of curiously mixed apprehension and pleasure. He came to stand on the other side of the hearth to Stephen and stood warming his hands, clearly not sure how to tell his news.

Sarah, who had an inkling of what was to come, came quietly to join them. "Well? Out with it, Tom! You have news of some sort, haven't you?"

Thomas eyed them uncomfortably. "Er . . . yes. In part good, in part bad . . . " he said, stalling.

Stephen too had a sudden premonition of what the news was. "Out with it then!" he commanded with a calm he did not feel.

Thomas looked helplessly at Sarah. "De Verais has begged leave to court Mistress Lucy!"

"And Mr Gleeson has agreed?"

"Oh, yes! He seems most happy about it — de Verais is a Huguenot, not a Catholic, you know. Mistress Lucy seems happy too!"

"They should deal excellently together!" Stephen said and meant it. He should have seen this possibility though. Poor Sarah. He had hoped that when all the fuss had died down she would have married de Verais. He glanced at his cousin but her face gave nothing away.

She was calmly asking her brother: "Will he take her away to France soon, do you think?"

"No, not yet awhile. There are troubles for Huguenots in France at the moment.

He will marry her here in the spring, I think."

"You could have a double wedding!" Sarah suggested.

"Oh, . . . yes." Thomas, looking uncomfortable again, sent his sister a warning look.

His embarrassment was so obvious that Stephen roused himself to take pity on him.

"I never was in love with Mistress Lucy," he informed his young cousin. "She is one of the nicest young ladies I know but if I had married her it would have been a marriage of convenience only. De Verais, I am sure, will take good care of her — and make you an excellent brother-in-law!" He spoke with sincerity and Thomas began to look happier.

"All the same, I should have preferred you as my other brother-in-law," he said honestly.

A situation I should not have been adverse to myself, Stephen thought wryly. But married to your own sister, not your wife's. Again he glanced at Sarah.

Her face was impassive in the firelight

and showed no sign of regret. Meeting his gaze, she said lightly: "What a pity we couldn't send you home with your fortune mended instead of a hole in your leg, cousin!"

They were all a little relieved when Burnet announced supper at that moment.

* * *

The next morning dragged past. After dinner Thomas went to call on Sir George but was shortly back with the news that Sir George, though better, was still not receiving visitors.

Stephen went for a short ride for exercise and soon found that his horse needed exercise more than he did. However he still felt that he should not be away from the house for long and returned to the stables early. Thomas was in the stable-yard giving instructions to a groom. The man moved to take Stephen's horse and Thomas called out: "Do you need anything from Lynn, Ansell? One of the men is going to ride into town to do some errands for Sarah."

"No, I think there is nothing I need,"

Stephen said slowly. "But how is the man with horses? Land-Lubber could do with a good workout — I have not been far enough lately to get the freshness out of him. A trip to town and back could be just what he needs."

"The lad knows his trade and would be proper careful of the horse, my lord. I can vouch for him." The head groom spoke without hesitation.

"Fine! Let the boy take him then."

The short afternoon soon began to turn dark and Stephen, mindful of Sarah's warning, took care to return from an exploration of the Priory ruins well before the light faded. As he walked across the hall he became aware of a swelling volume of noise coming from the servants' quarters. A woman was wailing and other voices were clamouring. The sounds became much louder for a moment, then died down again as a door was opened and closed. Burnet came into the hall and Stephen was startled to see how bemused and grief-stricken he looked. Seeing Stephen, Burnet made a visible effort to control himself and asked expressionlessly if Stephen knew

Lord Gerton's whereabouts.

"In the library, I think," Stephen replied briefly, not liking to question the man.

Burnet walked slowly along the passage, his steps dragging, and Stephen watched him with misgiving. Something was very wrong, he thought, and felt his stomach tense into a tight, hard lump.

Nor was he mistaken. A moment later Thomas came striding along the passage and even in the fading light Stephen could see that his face was as colourless as Burnet's.

"Ansell! Something dreadful has happened! One of the serving girls, returning from the village, has found Walt, the stable-hand who rode into Lynn this afternoon, lying in the lane. She thinks he is dead."

"Good God!"

"Walt is Burnet's nephew and he was riding your horse . . . " Thomas's eyes went anxiously to Stephen's face.

His words sent a stab of dread through Stephen, but not for his horse. He joined Thomas in the passage and, taking his cloak from Burnet, asked him directly:

"What kind of an accident was it?"

"I don't know, my lord. The girl didn't say. She's greatly upset and there's no sense to be got out of her."

As if to emphasise his words, a sob of female hysteria came from the servants' quarters.

"She was to marry Walt when he got on a bit, my lord."

"Come on!" Thomas broke in impatiently. "Does it matter how he met with his accident? He may still be alive and need our help."

Stephen nodded and followed him outside. In the lane, between the high hedges, it was now almost dark.

"Damnation! We should have brought a lantern," Thomas muttered but he did not pause. The pace he set was nearly a run and in the rear Burnet puffed after them, falling further and further behind.

Luckily they had a scant quarter of a mile to go. Stephen saw his horse first, standing nibbling the grass at the side of the lane. He had hardly moved since losing his rider, for they could see the boy lying only a few yards further on along the lane.

Thomas and Stephen knelt on either side of the boy but they did not have to touch him to know that he was dead. One look at his sightless eyes and the strange angle of his twisted neck told them all they needed to know. Stephen, as a formality, felt for a heartbeat but confirmed the obvious with a slight shake of his head.

Burnet, his breath coming in great panting gasps, came to stand at his nephew's feet. "He's dead, my lord?" he asked as soon as he could speak.

"I'm afraid so, Burnet. I'm sorry." Thomas looked up, searching for words to comfort the old man.

Stephen looked about him quickly, trying to make the most of the dying light. Another yard or two along the lane a broken bough hung down almost to the ground. If it had tangled with the boy's clothing it could have plucked the lad backwards from his mount. Could the boy really have been that careless? A rider not in complete control of his horse could have been taken under by a wayward animal but Walt had been an experienced stable-hand. Possibly he might have been daydreaming.

Getting to his feet, Stephen walked back to where Land-Lubber was standing docilely next to the hedge. His saddle bags did not appear to have been touched and his reins were in normal riding position, indicating that Walt had indeed fallen off backwards, and not been thrown over the horse's head.

"Ansell!" Thomas too had risen from beside the body. "Will you stay here while I take Burnet back and organise a stretcher party? I should not be long, for they must of a certainty be nearly ready by now."

"Of course." Stephen went to stand next to the body, now just a pale indistinguishable form in the gloom.

Had the lad met his death by pure misadventure or had he died because he had been riding his, Stephen's, horse? And if Walt's death had not been accidental had the murderer discovered yet that he had killed the wrong victim? Stephen peered into the darkness apprehensively but he could see or hear nothing.

He was not sorry when he saw a

lantern coming towards him from the direction of Banks House and he hailed the approach of the carrying party with relief. As the light came closer he quickly realised that he was wrong. Only one person was carrying the lantern and for one frozen moment he thought he was seeing the Black Monk. What he could see of the figure behind the glow of light seemed to be black-cloaked and black-cowled.

"Stephen?"

He recognised Sarah's voice and let out his breath with a rush of relief.

"Stephen! Are you all right? Oh, God, when I heard that someone had been killed and the horse was yours, I thought . . . "

The words came tumbling out and the lantern dipped dangerously.

Stephen went swiftly to her and took the lantern from her slack grasp. Holding it so that the light reached her face beneath the hood, he saw that her eyes were dark and glazed with dread. For once the icy control was gone and the fear changed to open relief as she looked back at him.

"Come, love, I'm all right!" he said gently. Afraid that she was going to faint, he put his free hand under her elbow. "You should not be here. It was Walt, the stable-hand, who was killed, not me."

"I know that now. But it was meant to be you, wasn't it? And I would have sent you to your death. I sent him to his death!"

Stephen felt her shudder uncontrollably.

"Pull yourself together, love!" He gave her a little shake.

"I am sure you were not the only one to request things from town this afternoon and I am just as much to blame by giving him my horse to ride."

"Then you do think he was killed deliberately, don't you?"

Sarah jerked her arm free of his supporting hand and fell to her knees beside the body.

Stephen bent forward with the lantern. By its light he could see something he and Thomas had missed in the gloom. Across Walt's throat was a thin discoloured line. It was too regular and too narrow to have been caused by the branch.

"Yes, I think he was," he said slowly.

Sarah had also seen the thin line. "What is it?" she asked curiously.

"The mark caused by whatever killed him — a cord stretched across the lane — the oldest trick in the book, I would say."

Stephen raised the lantern and examined the hedges on either side. There was no trace of a cord but the stems were particularly thick at this point, more than strong enough to hold a cord taut. The cord had been removed, so the murderer must already know he had killed the wrong person. It was wholly unlikely that Walt had been the intended victim. He said nothing of this to Sarah but shone the light onto the broken branch.

"We were expected to think that was the cause of the accident," he said soberly.

Sarah said nothing and he saw her eyes going from the dangling branch to the dead boy lying on the ground.

"The murdering swine!" she burst out suddenly, her voice trembling with helpless rage.

Stephen noticed more lanterns coming along the lane and, taking her arm again, he pulled her to her feet.

"Hush!" he said warningly.

Sarah made an effort to control herself. "Stephen, what are you going to tell them?"

"What do you want me to tell them?"

"Nothing. If they find out for themselves, so be it."

"The proper authorities should be told."

"If you tell the authorities now there will only be a great deal of fuss and trouble and they are not likely to find out who did kill the boy. His family will just be made more miserable to no purpose. The real murderer will be brought to justice shortly, I promise you."

"You are playing a very dangerous game in more ways than one."

"It is nowhere near as dangerous for me as it is for you!"

"That is different — I'm a man and used to danger. Besides I'm not inviting trouble as you are!"

"Sir George is not likely to take steps against me until after the wedding — he wants my dowry too much!"

"And after the wedding?"

"Care will be taken of that. But don't you see, you are inviting trouble by just being here. Won't you start for home tomorrow, Stephen? Please!"

"No. And here is not the time to argue about it. Come. I'm going to take you home now."

Stephen lifted her to sit sideways in the saddle, then, after a quick word of explanation to Thomas and Father O'Brien when they arrived, he led the horse forward into the darkness. He was unpleasantly aware that the lantern-light made them a well lit target but they reached the stables without mishap.

14

REACHING his bedchamber after a long evening playing piquet with Thomas, Stephen bolted his door and set the candle on the mantelshelf. The fire had died down too low to give out much heat and he wondered where Morris was to let it go unattended. Stephen kicked off his shoes and sat down feeling deadly tired.

All evening he had kept his thought away from Sarah and now he was too tired and muddled to know what to think. Had he seen love in her eyes for that short second or had it just been concern for a close friend? Reason told him it was the latter — and yet . . .

He should be feeling thankful that he was still alive. Without doubt it should be his broken body, not Walt's, now lying in cold state. Yet he felt he hardly cared. It was said that where there was a will there was a way but he no longer seemed to have any will power. The last few mouthfuls of mulled wine must have been too much on top of the evening's drinking. He should be undressing and getting into bed but a strange langour had invaded his limbs. It was not an unpleasant feeling once he had stopped fighting it and a few moments later his head dropped sideways and he slept.

He had no desire ever to awake but presently a searing pain in his right wrist shocked him into partial wakefulness. He opened his eyes to see flames leaping and burning above him. He could not remember dying but he supposed dully that the flames were the fires of Hell beginning to consume him.

"Water!" he muttered but the fire crackled louder. All the rain of Heaven cannot quench the fire of Hell. No, Mistress Fuller had said that to Sir George, not to him.

Gradually, as the pain made him more fully conscious, Stephen realised that somehow he had come to be lying on his bed and it was the bed hangings that were on fire. A piece of blazing material had fallen across his arm, setting fire to his sleeve. He tried to sit up and beat at the flames but his limbs felt like jelly and he found he did not have the strength to raise himself. With a supreme effort he rolled over, smothering the burning sleeve with his body as he did so.

Above him the bed burnt like a funeral pyre, the flames hissing and roaring as they licked the ceiling.

* * *

Sarah, lying fully dressed beneath the covers of the bed which had been recently occupied by her uncle, awoke feeling cold and tense. Curled up beside her, Tab slept with the unconcern of a kitten. Sarah was angry with herself. She had not meant to doze off and now, awakening with a start, she had the feeling that she had been sound asleep for a good while — by the diminished size of the candle she knew this was so. It was not surprising that she had fallen asleep, she supposed — this was the third time in succession she had lain awake half the night keeping watch on Stephen in his bedchamber on the opposite side of the corridor. Ever since he had knocked Sir

George from his horse she had been waiting for another attempt on Stephen's life. Walt's tragic death that afternoon had proved that one would come, she was sure.

Had Stephen come to bed while she slept, she wondered. The hour must be very late but possibly he and Tom were drowning their feelings together. The house was utterly silent — or was it? She sat up quickly, ready to fling off the covers and leap out of bed. Soft footsteps were coming along the corridor. For a moment they paused, seemingly outside her door, then there was the sound of a door being opened and closed very quietly. Stephen always did have a soft tread in spite of his height, she had noticed, but why bother tonight when he was supposed to be alone in the guest wing?

Sarah lay down again but not to sleep. If there was to be an attack made on Stephen that night it must come soon. She wished he would hurry up and bolt his door as he had done the previous couple of nights. The night was already far advanced: in a few hours it would be dawn. The last dawn before her marriage day. She shied away from this thought.

It was easier to be afraid for Stephen. While he was with her brother she judged him to be fairly safe. But now he was alone in his room? Something nagged uneasily at the back of her brain. Why didn't he bolt the door? Something was wrong somewhere, but what? Suddenly she knew. The footsteps had not been Stephen's — they had been too even. Stephen still walked with a slight limp and that evening as he had led Land-Lubber home she had noticed that it was more pronounced, probably from all the walking.

In one swift, silent movement Sarah was out of the bed and across to the door which she opened cautiously. The passage way was full of smoke and the smell of burning. Beneath Stephen's door a crack glimmered red, faintly at first but, even as she watched, growing brighter, and she heard the increasing crackle of flames.

For a split second Sarah stared at the glow in terror, then she rushed back to the bed and, tugging the covers off Tab, shook and pulled at the girl until she was standing shivering on the floor.

"What is it, my lady?" Tab gasped, pushing the hair out of her eyes.

"There's a fire in Lord Ansell's room. You must go and fetch Lord Gerton. Quick! Run!"

Sarah thrust the candle into the girl's hand and pushed her out of the door.

Following Tab into the corridor, Sarah did not waste time finding out if Stephen's door was bolted but, coughing, she felt her way along the wall in the smoky darkness until she came to the dressing-closet door. She turned the handle and the door opened immediately. The smoke in the closet was worse than out in the passage but through it she could see the bedchamber door outlined in the awful red glow.

In an instant she had the interleading door open and stood aghast at the inferno of blazing bed hangings. Her heart seemed to be in her throat, threatening to choke her, but she forced herself to go forward and look for Stephen in the pyre-like bed. The tester was almost burnt away and the covers were beginning to blaze. Choking and gasping, she seized an untouched pillow and beat at the flames. As she did so her brain registered a curious fact — Stephen was not in the bed. There was no time for relief or even to wonder where he was. As soon as the flames were down to a smoulder in one spot, another burning piece would fall from above, starting a fresh blaze.

* * *

Presently she became aware that Tab was beating away on the other side of the bed. Of Thomas there was no sign.

"Where is Lord Gerton?" Sarah croaked.

"I can't wake him, my lady. He's sleeping like one dead."

"Dead drunk, more like!"

Tab gave an hysterical giggle which ended in a choking fit. When she had control of herself once more she said laconically: "Lord Ansell is lying on the floor this side of the bed, my lady."

"Why didn't you say so before!" Sarah snapped. "Here, change sides with me."

Hardly daring to look for fear of what she might find, Sarah was very relieved to see Stephen lying on his back, apparently fast asleep. How he could sleep with all hell let loose around him she didn't know. One of his sleeves was slightly charred but he did not look to be in need of immediate attention, so she went back to fighting the fire.

Eventually the hangings were quite burnt away. The noise of the flames died down to an odd crackle as the wooden upper parts of the bed continued to smoulder. Above, the plaster of the ceiling was blackened but it did not look to have cracked. Sarah strained her ears for sounds of fire in the roof timbers but she could hear nothing except the wind outside. The bed seemed fairly safe at last, so, leaving Tab to watch it, she knelt down beside Stephen.

Mopping her streaming eyes, she saw he had not moved but was like one dead in his stillness. Sarah felt under his head and neck but could find no blood or injury. She tried shaking him gently without any result. Was he just drunk or — an icy suspicion suddenly gripped her — poisoned? However, looking at him, she was reassured. He looked too normal and he was breathing as if asleep. Then it came to her. Stephen was not poisoned but drugged.

Rising from her knees, Sarah bid Tab go and fetch Morris. "Tell him that something has befallen his master — that should bring him quickly. And you hurry too, please, Tab!"

Tab, nothing loath to leave the smoke-filled room, picked up a candle and ran. Sarah went across to the window and flung the casements wide. A gust of wind blew into the room, sending the smoke eddying. For a terrifying moment Sarah thought the bed was going to burst into flames again, so brightly did the smouldering bits glow, but mercifully there was little left to relight.

The air in the room was much clearer now. Sarah shut one half of the window and, picking up the remaining candle, took a careful look round the room. Near the bed Stephen's pipe was lying on the floor with its long stem broken into pieces. She knew that he did smoke sometimes before going to bed, because she had smelt the odd, lingering smell the tobacco left on several mornings recently. Whoever had started the fire had intended it to look as if Stephen had accidently set fire to the bed himself while smoking.

Sarah was having another less gentle try at wakening Stephen when Tab came back into the room.

"Where is Morris?" Sarah enquired sharply.

"I can't wake him either, my lady. I half pulled him out o' his bed but he ne'er so much as grunted!"

This did not really surprise Sarah. "They're all drugged," she said helplessly.

"Drugged, my lady? Why would they be that?"

"To keep them asleep," Sarah replied, regretting having spoken. "Go and see if there is any water in the dressing-closet, will you?"

Tab was more successful with this errand and returned with a nearly full ewer.

Sarah took it from her and splashed some water onto Stephen's face with her hand but still he did not move. Desperate now, she deluged his face straight from the jug. This had the effect of making him mumble unintelligibly but his eyelids remained closed.

"It's no good," she said to Tab. "I cannot waken him but we can't leave him lying here on the floor in a pool of water. He will die of cold. Somehow we will have to move him into one of the other rooms."

"Yes, my lady," Tab said obediently but wondering how they were going to manage this. Lady Sarah's shoulder was still sore, she knew, but perhaps between them they could carry Lord Ansell. She took the ewer from Sarah, slopping a little water onto the charred portion of Stephen's sleeve as she did so.

"Careful!" Sarah snapped. "He's wet enough already!"

But the smart of the water on his burnt skin penetrated Stephen's drugged state as no amount of shaking and splashing had done, With a grunt of pain he opened his eyes.

At first his vision was blurred and it was several moments before his sight started to clear. Vaguely he could remember flames around him and something to do with Hell but if this was Hell it was far too cold for his liking, he decided. The smell of burning was chokingly thick in the air and he was wet and cold. His leg ached with the cold and for some reason his wrist hurt as well. Perhaps if he moved nearer to the fire he would feel warmer. Without thinking further, he sat up.

The move was a mistake and he instantly regretted it. As soon as he lifted his head from the floor a violent throb of pain exploded inside it and an equally violent feeling of nausea seized him. He would have dropped back prone on the floor if Sarah had not held him up. Somehow he got his head in his hands and sat very still waiting for the nausea to subside. Presently he was able to lift his head and look round.

The view seemed strange. "Where on earth am I?" he asked thickly.

"Sitting on your bedchamber floor," Sarah told him succinctly, through teeth that all but chattered. Now that the worst was over she was shivering as much from shock as from cold. She had been kneeling behind Stephen holding him by the shoulders; now she let him go.

He twisted slowly round and stared at

her blackened face. "What happened?" he asked, still utterly bemused.

"There was a fire — you don't remember?"

"No, not really. Sorry. Must have a devilish hangover — my head is aching fit to burst!"

"Stephen, did you drink much last night?"

A fair bit, but not enough to have caused this, I would have thought." Yesterday seemed a long time ago.

"Did you smoke when you came to bed?"

"Smoke?" He was too tired for questions.

"Your pipe. Do try and remember. It's important."

Stephen did his best to try and think back. "No," he said finally. "I didn't light a pipe, I'm quite certain. I was too sleepy."

He was feeling sleepy again now, in spite of the cold and his various aches.

Sarah saw his eyes beginning to close and nudged him sharply. "Stephen, stay awake! You have been drugged, I think. So have Tom and your man Morris — we can't wake them at all. But you have to get out of this room you cannot spend the night on the floor."

Stephen looked regretfully at the bed. "Now I do remember a fire," he said, trying to concentrate. "It was all round me. I thought I was in Hell!"

"That you aren't is a miracle!" Sarah said sarcastically, then went on soberly: "Whoever drugged you intended you to be burned to death in that fire. How you got out of it alive I don't know. You must have a hard head for drugs, perhaps, or the Devil's own luck!"

Stephen was trying to sort out his vague memories. "I rolled off the bed, I think," he informed her. "Something was burning my arm and the pain woke me, I suppose. He looked at the charred mess of his sleeve ruefully.

"If you will get up now and go into another room I'll bind it up for you," Sarah coaxed. "Tab! Help me get Lord Ansell on his feet."

"Wouldn't it be better if I called one of the other man-servants, my lady?" Tab ventured.

Sarah had no wish for anyone else to be involved. "It would take too long — he would go back to sleep," she said briefly.

Stephen, his head exploding, had little to do with rising off the floor or with walking along the corridor to the room that had been his uncle's. Sarah and Tab each took an elbow and managed to half guide, half drag him to a chair in front of the fire. Once he was sitting still the throbbing in his head decreased and he tentatively opened his eyes again.

"That's better!" Sarah sounded relieved. "Tab, go and fetch me some salve and some clean linen to bind up his lordship's arm. Then perhaps we can get him to bed."

Tab went off and Sarah helped Stephen ease his arm out of the remains of his sleeve.

"You will soon mend, I think," she said, inspecting the burn on the inside of his wrist and forearm. "But your coat and shirt won't!"

"This time, rather them than me!" Although he was still feeling sleepy Stephen's head was beginning to clear. "How did you come to be awake at this hour and how did you know there was a fire? The smell of burning cannot have reached the other side of the house so quickly, surely?"

A faint blush spread under the soot smudges on Sarah's cheeks. "Call it feminine intuition, if you like," she replied evasively.

He would have called it something very different and would have questioned her further if Tab had not returned to the room at that moment. Sarah spread the ointment over the burn and, whatever it was, it did its work well, for by the time she had finished bandaging his arm the burn had almost ceased to smart. Stephen stretched out in the chair and settled back, watching her.

"Thank you," he said simply. His eyes were so dark with sleep they appeared nearly black in the candle-light. "You always seem to be on hand to minister to my hurts. What am I going to do without you after tomorrow?"

After tomorrow. Sarah hoped he had not noticed her sharply indrawn breath.

"You'll do what any sensible man would do in the circumstances — go and find a wife!" she told him firmly.

She hated herself for the hurt in his eyes but she knew she must force their relationship back onto an impersonal basis, else she would weaken in her resolution. She was relieved when his heavy lids drooped again. But he must not sleep yet — she had to get him to bed first.

"Stephen!" Sarah's voice recalled him once more. "You cannot go to sleep in that chair with only half a shirt and coat on!"

Stephen managed to open his eyes again and said with a slight smile: "I must look a queer sight! And it is rather cold, I admit!"

"Tab! See if you can find a nightshirt in his lordship's closet. The one Morris should have laid out on the bed would have been burnt to cinders. Would you like a hot drink, my lord? You must be frozen with all the water we poured over you."

Stephen was feeling cold in spite of the fire, but more from the formality of her tone and the closed expression on her face than from his own dampness. More wine would do nothing to warm him. However the thought of hot wine made him remember something. Looking down into the fire he saw again the spiced wine from the overset tankard go spilling across the hearth.

Aloud he said: "No, nothing to drink, thank you — I have had more than enough! But I think I can now tell you why I was not drugged completely unconscious like Morris and your brother were."

"Why?"

Struggling to get his thoughts in order, he said slowly: "We played cards tonight and just before we finished that new man, Sims, who took Burnet's place for the evening, offered to bring us some mulled wine — which he did. I took a mouthful or two of mine, but it was hot, so I put the tankard down on the hearth. Your cat came in with the man and later when it was brushing round my legs it knocked the tankard over. I drank the dregs which must have been pretty well laced but obviously I didn't get the full dose."

"So it was really Old Ironside who saved your life!" Sarah said in a curiously flat tone.

15

STEPHEN came upon Thomas slumped on the hall settle the next morning. Thomas's face was faintly tinged with green and he looked far from well. Morris had looked much the same. Stephen's own head was still aching, though nowhere nearly as badly as in the night.

"You look as if you are suffering!" he said not unsympathetically to Thomas.

"Lord!" Thomas said, closing his eyes. "I don't know when I felt worse! I hope you don't feel as awful, Ansell! — if you do I apologise!"

"My head has had years more practice than yours! However I have a confession to make — I must have been pretty far gone last night, for I fell asleep while smoking and I have burnt out one of your best beds!"

Another lie. There was going to be a great deal of explaining to be done when the truth finally did come out.

Thomas had opened his eyes wide. "Good God! You might have been killed! Were you hurt?"

"Slightly singed. I got out in time but the bed is ruined, I'm afraid."

Thomas gave vent to a laugh which caused him to hold his head. "Fanworth can deal with that — he can't wait to get his hands on this place! You can tell him about it this evening. Without as much as by your leave, he is coming to sup with us tonight, as he has some final arrangements to discuss — anyone would think he owns the house already! I'd better go and warn Sarah and Father O'Brien, I suppose." He rose reluctantly and wandered away in the direction of the kitchen quarters.

A moment later Sarah, leaning over the balustrade of the stairs, called to Stephen: "What is going on down there? Tom sounded upset, which isn't like him."

"I don't think he is feeling very well this morning!" he replied evasively, looking up. Sarah looked far from well herself, he thought. There were dark smudges of tiredness under her eyes. Also some change in her appearance too, though for the moment he could not place it.

"Nevertheless something must have happened to annoy him?"

"Sir George sent a message to say that he will sup with us this evening."

"Oh, is that all!" she said with attempted indifference.

"No doubt he means to bring your brother's title deeds," Stephen pointed out quietly, walking to the bottom of the stairs.

"If he does not I don't know when he does mean to!" Sarah's voice had dropped too and she straightened up wearily.

Stephen suddenly saw what caused the difference in her appearance. Instead of the stark black mourning she had always worn, the gown she now had on was of a misty dark grey. It fell in soft silken folds and its very colour seemed to absorb the aggressive brightness of her hair, leaving it glowing softly round her pale face.

Sarah saw his look and for a moment her eyes met his.

"My wedding-dress," she said quietly.

"It is very beautiful. The colour becomes you." Even to his own ears the words sounded formal and stilted.

Sarah smiled bleakly. "Sir George said he did not want to marry a woman who looked like a black crow, so . . . "

She stopped, seeing the anger flame in his face.

"How could he say a thing like that!" he asked savagely.

"That is his manner, I suppose. Stephen, don't upset yourself — it is too late."

"It is not too late!" he contradicted her angrily. "You cannot still mean to marry that madman!"

"I still mean to go on with the wedding, yes."

"But you can't!" Stephen said aghast. "It's not safe for you. If he did arrange that fire last night, and the death of the boy, there's no knowing what he may do to you once you are wed."

"That is a risk I shall have to take."

"Sarah, please won't you listen to sense? I know all the reasons why you think you must keep your vow, but I fear for your life if you marry Fanworth. How can I make you understand that I am not talking as a piqued lover — God forbid that I should force myself upon you! Surely you must realise that? But I could take you to our aunt and uncle. I am positive they would be only too happy to give you a home. I don't think Fanworth would be mad enough to follow you there." And as Sarah opened her mouth to protest he went on: "Yes, I do know what your brother would lose but he is plenty young enough to make his own fortune. I know he is your chief consideration, but . . . "

This time she did interrupt him.

"You are wrong, Stephen. I do have another consideration. Please believe me when I say I am not insensible to your concern for me, But . . . but there is something I have never explained to you . . . "

He looked at her, not really surprised. He had always felt she was holding something back. But he was surprised to see a faint flush outlining her cheekbones. "Lady Sarah?" someone called from beyond the gallery.

Sarah frowned, the little pucker making her look like brother. "The dressmaker. I must go. Meet me at the stables after dinner this afternoon and I will show you why I must go through with it."

With a brief rustle of silk she was gone.

When Stephen reached the stable-yard after dinner he found Sarah in the act of mounting Star Lady. Land-Lubber was ready saddled and, mounting, Stephen followed her out into the lane. Sarah's expression was not encouraging but Stephen ventured to ask: "Where are we going?"

"To Grimsby Hall, Sir George's house," Sarah replied shortly, urging Star Lady forward.

Stephen followed half a length behind, a position he kept until they were riding along the carriageway when he drew level with her to ask: "Is it safe to visit Fanworth like this? The sight of us together might provoke him to some fresh madness."

"I doubt it. He holds the ace, you see."

With this cryptic remark Sarah slipped swiftly from her saddle unaided and, tossing Stephen her reins, went to knock on the front door. Stephen paused to hitch the horses before mounting the steps in her wake.

The door was opened cautiously by a manservant Stephen instantly recognised as an older version of Sims, the man who had so successfully drugged them all the previous night. The man looked taken aback when he saw who the callers were and immediately informed them that Sir George was resting and did not wish to be disturbed.

"Never mind — you may convey our greetings to him when he wakes up! However it is Master Fanworth I wish to see. Pray conduct us to the nursery."

The man hesitated fractionally and, staring him straight in the eye, Sarah added: "I wish to know if he has fully recovered from his recent chill."

With a dubious look at Stephen the man opened the door wide enough for them to enter. "Certainly, my lady!"

There was an uncalled for insolence in the man's manner — like master, like servant, Stephen thought. But he had other things to occupy his thoughts as he followed Sarah and the man up the stairs and along a corridor to the back of the house. He had not known that Sir George had a son.

They reached the nursery door. Sarah dismissed the man and led Stephen into the room herself. The nursery was large and pleasant though the windows were barred. On the floor in front of the hearth a small boy was playing and one look at him told Stephen that he was not Sir George's son. His red hair gleamed brightly in the firelight.

Seeing Sarah, he jumped to his feet, crying delightedly: "Mama, Mama!"

She bent to pick him up, her face softening as she did so, but as she lifted the thin little body her expression was more one of pity than of maternal pride. His size was that of a two-year-old, but his face was far more mature, the face of a four — or five-year-old. The child's pale features lacked Sarah's healthy colour and freckles and his hair was less agressively red but his tawny eyes were hers, even to their slightly wary expression. For a moment Stephen closed his own eyes to blot out reality.

Sarah was speaking gently to the child: "You are better now, Johnnie?"

"Oh, yes, thank you, Mama! I am very well indeed! Papa says I may go to watch the big bonfire if there is one for Guy Fawkes Night!" His eyes were on the little package Sarah had brought for him.

"That will be nice," Sarah said absently. "Now you must make your bow to Lord Ansell who has come to see you, Johnnie, then you may have your treat." Smiling, she set him on his feet and handed the package to Stephen. "Will you give it to him please, my lord, while I speak to the nurse."

Johnnie bowed solemnly to Stephen and led him to a chair. Stephen seated himself and awkwardly lifted the mite onto his lap. Johnnie glanced up at him half fearfully but, seemingly reassured, he settled down quietly to unwrap the sweetmeats. Sarah went over to the night nursery door and called to the young girl who had withdrawn with a quick bob at their entry.

Sitting with the child on his knee, Stephen felt a numbing despondency steal over him; the child defeated all his arguments. The room was warm and peaceful with the fire crackling in the hearth and as the minutes passed Stephen forced himself to think. Johnnie had relaxed, child-like, and was now munching contentedly, except when he was shaken by a cough that racked his whole body. The situation had taken on a feeling of nightmarish unreality. The child unfortunately was real. He was nestling against Stephen's shoulder, a sticky dribble running down his chin and Stephen pulled out a handkerchief to wipe it.

Where the devil had the boy come from? Sir George certainly did hold an ace but there was always more than one ace in a pack. Now that he was thinking constructively instinct told Stephen that, in spite of the great likeness, the child was not Sarah's. However there was not the slightest doubt that he was a Perrington and that meant that he must be the young Earl's bastard. This did not help matters, for Sarah would protect them both to her last breath, if necessary. If the child was Thomas's surely he must know of its existence? No, it was possible that he did not.

But as soon as Sir George produced the boy Thomas would guess. Only by then it would be too late — Sarah would be wed.

Sarah came back with the nurse and lifted Johnnie from Stephen's knee.

"We must go now, Johnnie," she said gently. "I hope you won't be sick from eating all those sweetmeats at once!"

"Oh, no, Mama!" the little boy said earnestly. "Will you be coming to watch the bonfire?"

"Bonfire?"

"For Guy Fawkes Night, Mama!"

"Oh . . . we'll have to wait and see if there is one, won't we? Meantime, you be a good boy. Goodbye, my sweet." For a moment she buried her face in the soft curls, then, handing him to his nurse, she turned abruptly and left the room.

Johnnie seemed to accept her going as a normal happening, and after bowing to Stephen he began chattering to his nurse. Stephen gave the little boy a parting smile and went out, closing the door behind him. Once the childish little voice was cut off, the rest of the house seemed too silent. Sir George surely knew they were there but he made no attempt to see them or challenge their right to be there. The whole situation did not make sense.

Sarah was waiting for him in the hall but he would not risk questioning her there. Outside, the wind which had been blowing on and off for several days was rising to gale force and the noise was a rude contrast to the quiet of the house. Coherent speech would be too difficult, so without a word they mounted and rode down the carriageway to the lane.

However there were questions which had to be asked, so when they drew level with the ruins of Banks Priory Stephen took hold of Sarah's reins and said firmly: "I want to talk to you. There must be some shelter in the ruins."

He expected her to protest but she nodded and led the way in between the walls. Dismounting, Stephen assisted Sarah down and tied Star Lady securely to a rusted door-bolt. The broken walls shut out some of the force and sound of the wind and it was possible to talk without shouting.

Sarah seated herself on a fallen stone

and looked up warily at Stephen. She owed him an explanation, she knew, but that did not make it any easier. There was going to be an argument and somehow she had to get the better of it.

"So now you perceive the extent of my responsibilities!" She challenged him.

"No. Not entirely. That child is not yours!" His eyes held hers and he saw a flicker of — what, relief? — appear in them briefly.

But she said with forced scorn: "Cousin, you are too good to live! Everyone else can see that he is the image of me. Surely you don't doubt the evidence of your own eyes?"

"I'm not so naive that I don't realise he is a Perrington by-blow!" he told her cuttingly. "But that still does not make him your child. He could just as easily be your brother's." He frowned a moment, deep in thought, then added slowly: "Or, come to think of it, the red hair seemingly being an O'Brien not a Perrington characteristic, your cousin, Father O'Brien's. How in heaven's name did Fanworth come to have him?"

"He found him in a village over on the

Marshland. He was playing in the mud outside a cottage door."

"The devil he was!"

"Sir George recognised the relationship instantly," Sarah told him expressionlessly. "The couple who had custody of the boy could or would not tell Sir George anything of his ancestry, though they admitted he was not their child."

"They could hardly do otherwise — unfortunately!"

Sarah went on as if he had not interrupted her. "They said that the boy was brought to them by a distant relation from another village. They had thought the child was his but that he did not want his wife to know if its existence. They had recently lost their own baby, so they had taken the boy gladly. But he was sickly and difficult to rear and they were nothing loth to relinquish him when Sir George said he knew the boy's mother and would take over his keep. I think he must have paid them well to keep the matter as quiet as possible, for it has never become general gossip and, apart from the servants at the Hall, no one seems to know about him."

"An interesting little story, but it in no way proves that Johnnie is your child!"

Stephen thought he saw gratitude in Sarah's eyes but she looked away quickly and bent forward to pull at a withering weed. With added colour in her cheeks she said: "Sir George thinks the child is mine and John Carr's — that is why he is called Johnnie. But once we are wed Sir George will give out that Johnnie is mine and his. People will soon forget he was born before wedlock."

"He will name an unknown waif his heir just so that he can get his hands on, forgive me, your almost worthless property! The man must be completely crazy!"

Sarah sighed. "I have already explained to you why Banks House is so attractive to Sir George. He is greedy and cunning, I grant you, but in naming Johnnie he is really quite safe — you see, Johnnie is unlikely to live many months. He has a disease of the lungs — you have heard him cough — that he won't be able to fight off for much longer. You saw him well today but several times he has been so ill that I thought he would never get out of his cot again. That is why Sir George is insisting on marrying me now — if we wait until I am out of mourning he might lose his chief hold over me."

"If you refuse to marry him?"

"He will produce the child."

"Cannot you deny parentage?"

"And have him ruin Tom's chance of happiness with Anne or Father O'Brien's new appointment? I am certain that the Gleesons or the Howard family would not countenance such a scandal as Sir George would create. I told you before that he is completely ruthless when he wants something."

Baulked, Stephen said with bitter rage: "I agree with you! A man who can besmirch his bride's name to gain his own ends is a monster! I'll slit his throat for attaching such a scandal to your name!"

Sarah looked up at him in consternation. "Stephen, please, no! You'll only make things worse if you meddle — and you promised not to! I showed you Johnnie and told you the story so that you could understand."

"I understand that you are not going

to tell me whose child he is." Stephen said angrily.

"No I am not — you can think what you like!" Sarah flashed back with a spurt of temper equal to his own.

For a moment they glared at one another, then Sarah shrugged wearily and rose to her feet. "Don't let us quarrel, cousin. It could not make any difference if you did know whose child he is. Please just let matters alone. Tomorrow will settle everything for us all."

"For you, perhaps."

Sarah raised her eyes to his and in the fading light of the early winter dusk he saw her look of deep regret.

"I am sorry you ever had to come here, Stephen. Please believe me when I say I never meant to hurt anyone, least of all you." Sarah spoke so softly that the wind half drowned the words. Almost before she had finished speaking she had unhitched Star Lady and mounted without assistance.

On the ride back to Banks House Stephen ran through a fair variety of emotions — rage, hurt pride, defeat and depression — but he arrived knowing exactly what he had to do. If Sir George had not challenged him by the end of the evening he would call Sir George a coward to his face in front of his cousins as witnesses. The man would have no choice then but to call him out. Guest fighting sister's betrothed would place Thomas in a very uncomfortable position but the lad would survive. Perhaps one day Sarah would explain the real cause of the duel to him. This prospect did not cheer Stephen, for by that time he would either be dead or many miles hence.

16

ON her return to Banks House Sarah went straight to her bedchamber and flung herself face downwards on the bed. She had no thought of sleep, only to compose herself and gain a little strength for the coming night.

Stephen's refusal to believe that Johnnie was her child had touched her deeply but it had made the disagreement between them more bitter. If only he had accepted that the boy was hers and John's and had gone away mildly shocked and angry his hurts would have healed the quicker. She loved him for his trust and tenacity but it complicated her plans. She guessed he would try and force a duel on Sir George and if they fought tonight . . .

Her tired brain refused to think further. Worn out by lack of sleep and the emotional battle, she slipped into a dream-plagued sleep.

She was running along the bottom of

a ditch in near darkness, the high banks cutting off the moonlight. Somewhere behind her Sir George swore and cracked a whip. She stumbled along, sometimes slithering in the mud, sometimes being sucked back by it, and all the time Sir George was gaining on her. She came to a river-bank and was checked by the racing waves. Suddenly she realised John was standing on the far bank, his arms outstretched towards her.

"Sarah, you have come at last!" he called excitedly to her.

"I'm coming soon," she replied, looking at the wild water separating them.

"Come now. Quickly!" John pleaded. "The seventh wave will carry you here."

Why not, she thought, counting the waves. But even as the seventh wave swept towards her and she jumped Sir George reached her. He grabbed her by the shoulder and started to pull her back through the icy water. "No!" Sarah gasped as the scene became fogged and then faded.

With an effort Sarah opened her eyes and found Tab shaking her. She felt chilled right through but the shiver that seized her was more from the dream than the cold.

"My lady, you should have called me to light the fire," Tab said reproachfully.

"I didn't intend to sleep," Sarah replied truthfully.

She was thankful though that she had slept. She might be cold but she felt calm and purposeful. Like Stephen, she knew exactly what she was going to do that night.

* * *

Sir George handed his hat and cloak to Burnet and advanced into the hall. He looked fit and was far more richly dressed than usual — a dark puce satin suit gave him an almost dandified look. He was all politeness, apologising for coming to sup with them during what must be a busy time, but his stupid accident had caused a delay in the making of last minute arrangements.

Thomas, who had spent the afternoon sound asleep and was feeling his normal self again, forgot his irritation and assured Sir George that he was very welcome.

Sarah quietly joined the group. Her expression was serene as she curtsied to her betrothed. Sir George eyed her black brocade gown far more appreciatively than he had at the Gleeson's party.

"You are looking very beautiful tonight, sweetheart!" he said gallantly. His eyes roved over her and he looked satisfied with what he saw.

It was the first time Stephen had heard Sir George pay Sarah a compliment and, although he agreed wholeheartedly with the words, the look that followed sickened him. He barely had time to hide his distaste before Sir George turned to speak to him.

"I hear you had a slight mishap last night, Lord Ansell!"

"Mishap?"

"You were caught in a fire and narrowly escaped death, I believe," Sir George's gaze rested on Stephen's right wrist.

Instinctively Stephen smoothed the ruffles which hid the bandage. "News travels fast in the depths of the country! I trust you are fully recovered from your own accident, sir?"

"Completely, I thank you! Though I remember nothing of it, either before or after."

"Surely you must remember how it happened?" Stephen could not control the disbelief in his tone.

"My mind is a complete blank! It sometimes happens after a fall on the head, you know!" Sir George smiled at him blandly. "However they tell me you summoned help for me, my lord — for which I must thank you. I am ever in your debt!"

Stephen bowed, speechless, his mind refusing to believe what he had just heard. Sir George was far more clever than he had thought. The man had only to deny any knowledge of the insult to make it impossible for Stephen to fight him on that ground. One could hardly challenge a man who was so profound in his thanks.

In the entrance of the dining-parlour Burnet bowed, indicating that the meal was ready. Sarah moved forward and as she passed Stephen she said very softly: "You underestimated the man, I think, cousin!"

Father O'Brien joined them as they seated themselves at the table and as soon as everyone was settled Sarah asked him to say grace. The priest was the natural person to pronounce the prayer but Stephen guessed Sarah had endorsed this as she knew the formal Latin would annoy Sir George. A last act of defiance, he thought pityingly she could hardly be grateful for what she was about to receive.

The meal passed smoothly. Thomas and Sir George chatted amicably and Sarah and Father O'Brien were correctly polite. Two girls served the dishes ably, watched over by a wooden-faced Burnet, and to a stranger the scene would have shown a pleasant family meal. The tension was there though, unnoticed by Thomas and seemingly unnoticed by his guest. Stephen remained as silent as courtesy allowed.

When the last of the dishes had been removed and Sarah was about to withdraw Thomas rose suddenly to his feet.

"Before you go I would drink your health, sister, in thanks for our happy years together. May you and Sir George continue to be happy here and at Grimsby Hall!" He raised his goblet. "To my sister!" he said simply.

"To the Lady Sarah!" the three other men pronounced.

For a lingering moment Sarah looked at her brother's pink and earnest face, her own becoming mask-like. If she had been pale before she was porcelain white now, but after the moment of hesitation she inclined her head in acknowledgement, then rose and swept the company a curtsy.

"Thank you," Her voice was quite controlled. "Now I will bid you all good-night — you will understand that I have preparations to make for tomorrow."

Sir George leapt to his feet to open the door for her.

"Why, yes, sweetheart! The preparations for the ceremony are all complete and I have at last got Lord Gerton's title deeds finalized. Certainly you must make ready for your part in tomorrow but see you do not stay up too late — my bride must be as fresh as a daisy!" He raised her hand to his lips and kissed it with gusto. "Till our next meeting, sweetheart!"

Sarah, withdrawing her hand, sank into a curtsy that was almost mocking in its depth. "Thank you, sir. Till our next meeting," she echoed calmly and walked through the door.

Sir George's show of ardour towards Sarah caused gall to rise in Stephen's throat again. He tossed off the remains of the wine in his goblet, then hastily schooled his expression, suddenly aware that Father O'Brien was watching him.

Sir George returned to the table, drawing out a packet of papers from the inside of his doublet as he did so. He dropped them down in front of Thomas.

"Your deeds, my lord!" He picked up his goblet. "I give you the Lord of Gerton Hall, gentlemen!"

Stephen reached mechanically for the wine bottle, glad of a distraction that removed Father O'Brien's gaze from his face. Thomas was looking idiotically disbelieving.

When they finally rose from the table, Thomas clutching the precious packet of papers, Stephen did not accompany him and Sir George to the parlour but turned aside to follow Father O'Brien into the library. An evening spent in the priest's company was the last thing he desired at the moment but Father O'Brien was his only hope. As the Black Monk he might know something which could be used against Sir George and thus stop the wedding.

The library was in darkness except for a glow from the dying fire and Stephen had to fetch a taper to light the candles. Aware of the priest watching him speculatively, he said curtly: "They will have much to discuss and better alone."

He walked over to the window where the curtains were still drawn back on either side of the black arch and reached out to draw them but for several moments his hand stayed arrested on the faded brocade. Outside, at the far end of the house, the lantern that lighted the way to the stables had been lit and was hanging from its bracket, swaying dangerously in the wind. Directly beneath it was the black-clad figure of Thomas talking to a man that Stephen recognised as the head groom. Rubbing round the Earl's legs was Old Ironside. As Stephen watched he saw the groom nod as if in agreement and turn away out of sight towards the stables. Thomas bent to ruffle the cat's fur, then walked swiftly out of the circle of light and vanished into the darkness. Old Ironside stretched and followed more sedately.

Stephen drew the curtains squeaking across the rod. His thoughts went back to the evening when Sarah, dressed in her brother's clothes, had jumped laughingly out of the window. Much had happened since that night, most of it bad. That's what you get for tampering with witchcraft, he thought, half seriously.

Father O'Brien, on his knees before the hearth as he coaxed the fire back to life, asked abruptly: "What made you stay for the wedding, my lord?"

Stephen swung round at the suddenness of the question.

"Why? — because my cousins asked me to stay!" He forced his tone to be light.

Father O'Brien continued as if he had not heard Stephen. "You are perfectly fit

enough to ride now, I think, my lord?"
"Oh, perfectly!"
"Yet you stay to attend a ceremony which is repugnant to you?"
"One's duty is often repugnant!"
Father O'Brien raised his eyes to Stephen's face. "Is it really your duty to watch the young woman you love marry a man you despise?"
Stephen stared back at him. For the second time that night he was speechless.
Father O'Brien went on quietly: "Remember, the onlooker sees most of the game, my lord certainly more than the players. I have known for some weeks that you are in love with the Lady Sarah."
"It is not always possible to order one's feelings, Father!" Stephen snapped defensively. He was in no mind to receive a lecture on his failings from the priest.
"Sometimes it is not possible to order them at all, but to love when the way is barred leads only to heartbreak."
"As you would know, Father!"
"As I well know." The old man looked away to watch the now leaping flames. "Oh, yes, I have loved, my son. A few

years back I loved a woman unto death, despite my calling. And the years since have been empty . . . ”

At the back of Stephen’s mind something stirred. He had no wish to rake up painful memories for the old man but the tale might provide useful information. The priest said that a few years ago he had loved. Had he loved from afar or had the result of his loving been Johnnie?

He said carefully: “Would it ease you to tell me about it, Father?”

For a moment Father O’Brien hesitated, then seating himself in a chair he began his tale.

Some years ago he had been called secretly to a distant village to hold a Requiem Mass for a farmer. After that he had at odd times held a surreptitious mass at the village and afterwards he had often helped the farmer’s widow, Mary Grey, with the financial management of the farm, as her brother-in-law, piqued at not inheriting, had refused her any aid.

Father O’Brien had welcomed having work of value to do again and the visits to the farm became the highlights of his life. Gradually his friendship with the widow had deepened. He had tried to concentrate on the spiritual guidance he was providing for the villagers and all might have remained innocent had not a blizzard made it impossible for him to leave the farmhouse one night — By the next morning two lonely people had found all the bodily comfort they needed.

They had continued in the new relationship, unworried that Mary might conceive. Her marriage of more than twenty years had been barren and now she was almost past the age of child-bearing. However God had decreed otherwise and Mary became pregnant. Father O'Brien's reaction had been one of deep alarm, not only because they could keep their relationship secret no longer but because Mary's age made having a first child highly dangerous — fears that proved to be only too well founded. Father O'Brien had engaged the best midwife he could find; after that he could only pray.

About the time the birth was expected he had been confined to bed by a severe attack of winter ague. When he had been well enough to go to the farm he had found it deserted. In the village they told him the Widow Grey had died suddenly more than a week before. When he had paid the midwife she had confirmed that the baby, a boy, had died with its mother.

Father O'Brien had held one last mass, then never returned to the village.

"Mistress Fuller guessed that the brother-in-law had slipped the baby's corpse secretly into the coffin before the burial," Father O'Brien ended sadly.

Stephen, whose interest had flagged at the death of the child, sat upright. "Mistress Fuller?" he asked sharply.

"Aye. She was much sought after as a midwife and a healer before the tale that she was a witch went around. You yourself have experienced her powers of healing!"

Stephen's mind was working at top speed now that there was a slim hope left — for some reason better known to herself Mistress Fuller might have lied about the death of the child.

To Father O'Brien he said: "Indeed I have! And you put me in mind that I have never properly thanked her for what she did for me. I am quite certain that without her help I should now be dead. The hour is late but tomorrow there may be no time and I leave at dawn the next day." He got abruptly to his feet. "Please excuse me for a while, Father, and thank you for confiding in me. I hope that time may ease your loss," he added awkwardly.

Outside the house he was surprised at the force of the wind. In the open, between the house and the stables, it was like fighting a living thing which came clawing at him out of the darkness. It was the worst gale he had experienced on land and, unlike gales at sea, there was a different menace of dust and other small objects which came hurtling at him. The flame of the lantern had blown out, so in darkness and with eyes half closed against flying grit he felt his way round to the back of the stables. Beneath the door which led to the rooms where the Fullers now lived there was a thin bar of light.

It was as if Mistress Fuller had been awaiting him, so swiftly did she answer his knock. She was fully dressed, he noticed, while her brother seemed to have gone to bed. The room was empty except for Mistress Fuller and him, while from the inner room came the sound of snoring. Mistress Fuller bade him enter and he crossed the threshold, closing the door behind him to shut out the wind.

"The hour is late but before I leave I would thank you for saving my life."

He held out a purse but she refused it with a quick shake of her head.

"A life for a life," she said with simple dignity.

Stephen bowed. Then, holding her eyes with his, he said: "And I would know the truth about a life."

"Whose life?"

"The life of the child Mistress Mary Grey bore some years ago. She died, but the baby, was he alive or dead when you left the farm?"

"'E was alive — just. But I saw death in 'is face. 'E would ave been dead within the hour, 'e was so small and weak. I wrapped 'im and left 'im beside 'is mother."

"You were so certain he would die

that you told Father O'Brien that the baby was dead?"

The old woman shrugged. "Was it not kinder to tell 'im that 'is child was dead than to raise 'ope in 'is mind? Oh, yes, I knew the child was 'is, though 'e didn't tell me so. 'E was suffering enough for 'is sins."

"And now others are suffering. For all the baby was so weak and small, he lived. He is still alive — I saw him this afternoon."

For a moment the old woman's eyes widened, then they slid away towards the flickering flame of the tallow candle. "I saw death in 'is face," she repeated stubbornly. "And I still say 'e will die — very soon."

It was Stephen's turn to shrug. "At the moment he lives and I will have to tell the Father so."

He turned to go. He did not relish the task of telling the priest that his son lived, as the child had so little time. What Sarah's reaction would be was not hard to guess, but with the priest's help he would yet prevent the wedding. It would be hard on the old man but it was right that he should pay for his sins, not Sarah.

Mistress Fuller dragged her eyes away from the tiny flame and pulled the door open for Stephen. "'E will die," she said and the howl of the wind seemed to echo her prophecy as he walked back to the house.

Father O'Brien was still sitting as Stephen had left him, staring into the fire and making no pretence of working on the papers spread on the table. He looked up listlessly when Stephen entered and noting his windblown appearance said politely: "An evil night, my lord."

"Evil indeed, Father. And not just the weather!" Stephen stopped and, suddenly conscious of his untidiness, ran his fingers through his hair. Short of blurting it out, he had no idea of how to break his news to the priest. He tried again: "A great evil is about to be done . . . "

The sound of loud voices in the hall made Stephen break off. Tension like a clamp gripped his stomach and he turned towards the door.

Behind him the priest asked quietly: "The evil you fear, my son?"

"I think not."

Stephen strode to the door and, opening it, looked along the passage. Burnet had just opened the door of the small parlour and a strange man stood in the doorway, his chest visibly heaving. His panting voice came clearly down the passage.

"Master! Come quick! The men from the village are attacking the windmill. They're hacking it to bits! And the Black Monk is there with them!"

For the space of a few seconds there was silence, broken only by the man's wheezes. Then with a great oath Sir George burst out of the parlour, pushing the man aside and roaring for his cloak and sword as he did so. Burnet handed him these and was rewarded by another string of oaths. Sir George ignored Thomas who had followed him into the hall and a moment later the side door crashed shut. A heavy silence settled on the house.

In the library doorway Stephen stood in quick thought. Father O'Brien was in the room behind him, so it was not he who was the Black Monk. As Stephen's eyes met Thomas's down the length of the passageway he knew what he should have guessed sooner. The figure he had seen talking to the groom earlier had not been Thomas but Sarah — the loving actions of the cat should have told him that. If he was to prevent Sir George from killing Sarah there was no time to be lost.

With an oath almost as profane as Sir George's Stephen felt for the door handle behind him. As he pulled the door shut he heard Father O'Brien say: "May God go with you, my son!"

Stephen smiled grimly. There was going to be a great fight between God and the Devil before the night was out.

17

THOMAS called Burnet to bring his riding boots and cloak and Stephen, after asking Burnet to inform Morris to bring the same for him, seized Thomas by the shoulders and propelled him back into the parlour, shutting the door behind them.

Thomas squirmed out of Stephen's grip and looked questioningly at him.

"Why did you let Sarah go out tonight?" Stephen asked curtly.

A wary look came over Thomas's face. "She said she . . . "

"Don't try to bamboozle me, lad!" Stephen broke in. "I know that Sarah is the Black Monk! Where did she go tonight?"

"I don't know. We quarrelled about it long ago and she stopped telling me what she was doing."

"You must have known all the same!" Stephen longed to shake Thomas.

"Yes, but . . . " Thomas bit his lip,

then started again with a rush. "It all started as a joke. I dressed up a couple of times to scare people but Sarah made me stop. Then after John Carr was killed she started to dress up herself, but she led the villagers to attack Fanworth's drains, which I never did. I kept quiet for a while, thinking it would help her work off her grief, but when she nearly got caught once I begged her to stop. She told me to go to the devil and we had a flaming row! I told her I wasn't going to help her any more — if she wanted to go on and get herself killed that was up to her."

That was probably exactly what Sarah did want, Stephen thought sadly, but he made no comment.

Thomas went on: "Since then she has never told me when she was going out. I knew she went, of course, and we quarrelled about it every so often. After Fanworth nearly killed her that night I made her promise not to go out alone again. But tonight was her last chance — and I didn't want to quarrel with her on her last night at home. I knew Sir George would be here, safely out of the way."

Thomas looked miserably at his cousin and Stephen's anger died away.

"Well, he isn't safely out of the way now," he pointed out. "Somehow we have got to get Sarah away before Fanworth finds out her identity." He nearly said: "Before Fanworth kills her," but there was no sense in being cruel. He went on: "If he does discover that she is the Black Monk I hate to think what he will do to her. I will go and try to keep them apart. Fanworth has a good start on us but with luck he won't find her straight away. You had better go to the Priory ruins and wait for her in that room she uses — yes, I found it when I looked round the ruins one day. I will try and make her go there and you must get her home as fast as possible. Use force if necessary!"

They both smiled bleakly, knowing Sarah would not suffer herself to be spirited home without strong resistance.

There was a tap on the door and Burnet entered with the Earl's cloak, hat, boots and sword. Stephen left him to dress and went out into the hall. Morris appeared a moment later, his face anxious.

"Let me come with you, my lord," he begged as he handed Stephen his sword.

For a moment Stephen was tempted, then he shook his head.

"Not tonight, friend! I have a personal score to settle which can best be dealt with alone!" he said softly.

Thomas and Stephen parted when they came to the ruins. Riding on alone, Stephen came to the top of the rise on which the Priory was situated and saw that the messenger had told the truth. There was a glow in the sky which penetrated the thinning hedges. The lurid redness could mean only one thing — fire. Oh God, don't let me be too late, he prayed as he covered the remaining distance. Stephen avoided the Hall and rode on along the lane until he found a gate. Entering the field, he reined up short, Land-Lubber tossing his head and snorting through his nostrils at the awesome sight.

The windmill was an inferno. The wooden walls of the tower belched flames which had spread to the great sail arms. The canvas sails had already been consumed but the flames blazed heavenwards in the form of a monsterous fiery cross, the four arms being neatly stuck, one pointing to the sky, one to the ground and the other two outstretched on either side. The roar of the fire could be heard even above the sound of the wind and sparks streamed overhead like the tail of a comet.

Land-Lubber shied back towards the hedge and Stephen, slipping from his back, led him into its shelter and deemed it wise to tether him securely for once. Stephen could see no sign of Sir George or Sarah. A group of men were huddled well back from the fierce heat of the fire — there was nothing they could do about it but stand and watch uneasily. Stephen picked his way through the stubble towards the men standing etched by the flames. The scene was as light as day.

"Where is Sir George?" Stephen asked a man he recognised as Fanworth's steward.

"He's gone chasing the Black Monk, your honour. When Sir George arrived here the Monk were just riding away.

away. Sir George went straight after him. Mad as the fire he were!"

Stephen swore. He had hoped to catch up with Sir George before he got to Sarah. Now there was little hope of that.

"Which way did they go?" he asked tersely.

The steward shrugged. "That way, I think, your honour." He pointed across the field towards the house. "There was men everywhere — wreckers running away and my men chasing them. The fire were just starting and I was looking to see if the windmill could be saved, but in this wind it were impossible."

Stephen nodded and turned back towards his horse. It passed through his mind that none of the saboteurs seemed to have been caught. There was too much sympathy for their cause, he hoped.

He freed Land-Lubber with a soothing word. Swinging himself up into the saddle, he froze, every hair on his body rising. A small white figure was coming across the ground from the direction of the house. Too small for a man, it crept across the field towards him. For a long moment he thought he was seeing the real Priory ghost, then, as the form stumbled, fell headlong and scrambled upright again, he realised it was a human child. In a sudden blaze-up from the windmill he recognised Johnnie.

Not without difficulty Stephen got the unusually restive Land-Lubber to sidle across the field to the child.

Johnnie peered up at him. "Papa?" he asked tentatively, the wind snatching the words away, but Stephen guessed his question.

Dismounting beside the small boy, he shook his head. "No, Johnnie, I'm not your papa. I'm Lord Ansell — I came to see you this afternoon, do you remember? Whatever are you doing out here at this time of night?" And in this kind of weather, he added mentally.

"I came to see the bonfire. Papa said there was going to be a bonfire for Guy Fawkes Night and that I might see it. Where is Papa? I want him!" The words ended in a bout of coughing.

Of course, it was almost Guy Fawkes Night, and Stephen could still remember the thrill of the big bonfires held in his childhood to mark this night, but what could Sir George be thinking of to even mention allowing Johnnie to watch? Come to think of it, would Sir George with his Parliamentary leanings allow a bonfire? Without difficulty, he answered his own questions, and felt physically sick — letting the delicate boy out in the cold, damp night air would be a good way in which to hasten his end.

Bending down so that Johnnie could hear him above the wind and taking hold of one cold little hand, he said: "Johnnie, your Papa isn't here and what you see is not the bonfire for Guy Fawkes — it is the windmill burning down. Come, I will take you up on my horse and we will ride back to the house. It is too cold for you out here."

"I want Papa!" Johnnie shouted, the words ending in a wail.

Stephen looked desperately towards the house. He was losing time but he couldn't leave the child here. Where the devil was his nurse? Surely she must guess where he had run off to?

"Let us go and look if he is in the

house, then," Stephen said, letting go of the child's hand to pick him up and sit him on the horse.

"No! Papa said I might watch the bonfire!" Johnnie was not going to be cheated of his promised treat and with a sudden twist he squirmed away from Stephen and began to run across the field towards the fire.

Still restive, Land-Lubber shied at the small white form and reared up. Stephen, grabbing at the reins, realised the horse was still too nervous to stand alone and was forced to lead him back to the hedge. By the time he had tied the horse securely Johnnie had gained a good start and had almost reached the men who were still standing watching the fire.

Stephen was halfway across the field when above the noise of the wind he heard a cracking sound. Looking up, he saw with horror one of the charred vanes bend in the gale. Amid a great burst of sparks it broke off at the boss and came hurtling down at a slant, carried sideways by the force of the wind. In its path a fascinated Johnnie stood still, watching it.

A man saw the child and leapt to grab him but he was sent spinning as the tip of the sail frame caught him a glancing blow. The next instant the still burning frame had thudded into the ground and Johnnie had vanished beneath it.

By the time Stephen reached the spot the men had dragged the smouldering frame aside. It took only a glance at the poor pulped little body to know that Mistress Fuller's prophecy had come true. The small face, untouched by the crashing woodwork, still smiled in excited wonder. At least he had not suffered, Stephen thought numbly, turning aside. But if he ever got his hands on Sir George *he* would surely suffer, Stephen vowed.

To the men he said curtly: "Take him back to the house. I will find Sir George and tell him what has occurred."

"It weren't no fault of ours," one of the men muttered.

"I know that and will tell him so. Are you all right?" he added, as the man who had been knocked down by the falling frame struggled to his feet, rubbing his shoulder.

"Yes, m'lord. I'm sorry . . . "

"You did what you could." There was no time to be wasted in words — too much time had passed already.

Mounted once more, Stephen turned his back on the fire and picked his way to the house. The stable-yard was empty, though lanterns flickered in the wind. He went on round to the front of the house, which he at first thought was equally deserted. Only just in time he noticed a movement in some tall shrubs growing near the front door. The split-second warning gave him sufficient time to drop flat on his horse's neck before a man with a pistol in each hand stepped out of the bushes and fired at him. The shot went through the brim of Stephen's hat, so close that he fancied he could feel it pass along his back. Recovering from the shock, he dug his spurs into Land-Lubber's flanks and as he bore down on the man he got his right foot free of the stirrup. The toe of his boot caught the man a vicious blow under his chin as he was in the act of changing pistols from hand to hand. The pistol discharged harmlessly and as the man went staggering back Stephen saw it was Sims, the man who had tried to burn him in his bed.

Stephen galloped straight on down the drive, his heart pounding. Sir George must have guessed he would come after him and had left the man to ambush him. Time was too short to worry if there was anyone else lurking in the darkness. More important was the direction in which Sarah was leading Sir George. The Priory ruins was the most obvious choice but was that where Sarah would go? Suddenly he remembered the sluice gates in the Sea Wall. It would be just like Sarah to attempt one more last act of defiance.

One final act. Clearly, as if he could see into her mind, Stephen realised Sarah's plan of revenge. The odd slips of the tongue she had made fitted into place too well for there to be any doubt. The time in the garden when she had said that she would soon be dead to him; he had not taken her literally, yet she had meant exactly that, he now realised. And when he had accused her of planning to kill herself she had rightly denied it — she was planning to have Sir George kill her. When he discovered he had killed his betrothed before the wedding had given him her dowry, that would be Sarah's ultimate revenge.

Stephen rode straight on past the Priory ruins. If Sarah had gone there Thomas would stop anything drastic. As he left the protection of the lane a fresh pelter of sleet hit him.

The strength of the wind was much greater out on the open marsh and it was not long before his hat went flying away. The wind drummed in his ears until it blotted out all thought — for which Stephen was not sorry.

How he found his way across the marsh he could not afterwards recall but presently he became aware that he was riding along the bank of the river. The moon, full out behind the clouds, gave enough light for him to see the wind-torn ripples on the black water. The river gave him a sense of direction and he decided to follow it. It might not be the most direct route with its many meanders but it was the most certain.

At last Stephen saw he was nearing the

Sea Wall. The river was dyked high on his left and Land-Lubber was struggling through increasingly large pools of water. Stephen peered up at the dyke, trying to judge if it was still strong enough to ride on. He decided not to risk it but it was clear that if Land-Lubber carried him much further they would both be swimming. Coming to a fair-sized patch of ground which was still well above the flood waters, he reluctantly dismounted. There was nothing to tether the horse to, so he could only knot up the reins and hope that Land-Lubber had forgotten the fire sufficiently to stand calmly and not wander.

Stephen scrambled up the muddy side of the dyke and was glad he had not tried to ride along it. The river was very high and quite large waves, lashed up by the wind, were eating away at the side of the dyke. In one or two places he had to jump over water spilling right across the bank. He tried to increase his pace, driven on by the fear that he would not reach the sluice gates before the dyke gave way, but the sheer force of the wind held him back. It buffeted the breath from his lungs and an extra strong gust almost sent him staggering over the edge.

Splashing through a spill too broad to jump, Stephen was relieved when his boots crunched on mortar at the far side. A moment later he reached the sluice gates. The gates were firmly closed in their bed, dividing the river flood from the raging sea. In spite of the waves pounding at it, the structure seemed sound enough and Stephen guessed that the dyke bank would give way before the gates did.

It took him the best part of a minute to realise that he was quite alone. The mortar structure which held the gates in place was pale and shadowless in the dim light and it was empty of anyone but him. Stephen had been so certain that he would find Sarah and Sir George here that for a time he stood irresolute. A heavy shower that was more sleet than rain resoaked his flying hair and sent fresh drips down the neck of his cloak. The icy wetness running down his back stirred him. There was no point standing about getting wetter and wetter.

He was sure that the closing of the gates was Sarah's doing, though it would be far beyond her strength to do it herself. Probably she had got the village men to shut them before they had gone to attack the windmill. No matter, it would provide the perfect goad for getting Sir George to attack her. The more he considered the idea, the more certain Stephen became that Sarah would have led Sir George here — but where were they? Had he been too late? But then surely he would have passed Sir George on the way. Unless . . . A hideous fear seized him. If they had gone too near the edge an extra-large wave could have swept them away.

Spluttering as the spume from a high breaking wave blew into his face, Stephen walked to the edge of the Sea Wall and looked down. The quick glance he took before another great wave crashing into the structure sent him leaping back was enough to convince him that nothing could live, not even for a moment, in the wildly boiling sea. If Sarah and Sir George had gone that way they would not be returning.

Defeated, Stephen was about to retrace

his way back along the dyke when something far to the right along the Sea Wall caught his eye. Instantly he halted — there had been a flash in the darkness, he was sure. It could just be phosphorescent spray but he had to be certain. Eyes straining, he stared along the wall. He could hear nothing above the crashing of the waves and the fury of the wind but presently he saw it again in the darkness — the almost unperceivable spark of steel upon steel.

Fanworth must have driven Sarah along the wall and unless something was done quickly they would both be swept off and drowned by the sea.

18

STEPHEN began to feel his way along the wall step by step. He bunched up his cloak under his arm to prevent the wind tugging at it — he would have removed it altogether but the wet seemed to have jammed the clasp. Even so, he could not stand upright for the force of the wind and had to bend forward into it. He was becoming very wet, though whether from spray or rain he could not tell. The walk seemed to take hours. Once a crevice and an extra strong gust of wind nearly sent him tumbling into the sullen black flood. Great waves were breaking against the seaward side of the wall and old Mistress Fuller's words passed through his mind. He began to count each wave as it broke . . . Four . . . five . . . six . . .

He was practically within touching distance of the nearest combatant before he could make out who was who. Sarah had managed to rid herself of her cloak and was driving her betrothed slowly along the wall. Sir George, his lips agape in a panting open-mouthed scowl, seemed to be biding his time. He was no match for Sarah's speed and finesse but he had the sense to know that the slim figure must soon tire, so he contented himself with simple defence. The clouds parted for a moment and Stephen caught a glimpse of the man's eyes, cold and hate-filled, as he waited for his chance.

Somehow the mad duel had to be stopped before murder was done. Unmindful of the raging elements, Stephen stepped forward to pull Sarah back, by the scruff of the neck if necessary. As he moved Sir George saw him. A look of disbelief appeared on his face and his defence wavered. Sarah noticed his attention falter and, quick to seize her chance, she lunged.

If the point of Sarah's sword had reached its target Sir George would have died from the thrust, but even as the sword flashed forward he disappeared in a wall of breaking water and a thunderous crash. Sir George and the section of the Sea Wall on which he had been standing vanished into the raging sea and water began to pour through the gap. Stephen, who had seen the giant wave come racing along the wall a split second before it broke over Sir George, grabbed Sarah round the waist and pulled her back. Both were deluged by falling water and had to struggle to maintain their balance on the shaking wall.

Suddenly Sarah pulled herself free from Stephen, turned and thrust at him. The attack was so unexpected that he barely had time to jump backwards out of reach. Sarah screamed something at him but the words were lost in the the general uproar of the storm. Seeing the glaze of blind rage on her face, Stephen knew there was nothing personal in the attack — cheated of her revenge, she was venting her pent-up feelings on the nearest object, him.

"Sarah! Stop it! 'Tis I, Stephen!" he yelled at her but from her unchanged expression he knew she had not heard.

Stephen was forced to keep backing ignominiously away. Sarah was too good a swordswoman to ignore and there was no question of his drawing his own sword on her, though his hand itched to bring her back to her senses with the flat of it. Had they been on firm ground he would have done just that.

"Tire out quickly, my love!" he prayed.

Sarah drove him back almost to the sluice gates. Glancing down, Stephen could see that the water trapped on the landward side of the wall was boiling nearly as violently as the sea on the other side and he guessed that the dyke containing the river had also collapsed. He could sense rather than hear the water rushing through a gap. Oh, my God, how are we going to get back across it, he thought wildly.

He did not have time to speculate. Sarah stumbled in a wash-away crack and pitched forward, almost at his feet. Stephen's long arm shot out and grabbed her wrist with such force that her fingers lost their grip on her sword hilt and she dropped it. Gently Stephen lifted her to her feet.

A moment later he realised that he would have done better to have left her lying in the mud, for she seized on him like a wild cat. Still in the grip of ungovernable temper, she beat and tore viciously at his face and clothes. Stephen held her off as best he could, heartily thankful for his long reach. When at last it became born on Sarah that she was getting nowhere with her hands she changed her tactics. A forceful kick landed just above Stephen's left knee, right on the scar of his recent wound. With a gasp of pain he went staggering backwards.

As he recovered himself, he saw for the second time that night a giant wave come racing along the wall towards him. This time it did not break short and Stephen only just managed to grasp Sarah round the waist again before the wave burst over them, flinging them through the air as if they were droplets of spray. Even as they fell Stephen felt thankful that they had been knocked forward and not sucked back into the sea as Sir George had been — though they were as likely to drown in the flood waters as in the sea. They hit the water with a thudding splash that knocked most of the breath from their bodies and went plunging down into the icy blackness.

The water was not all that deep and

submerged tussocks of grass and reed began tearing at their faces as they were swept along by the force of the river water pouring through the breached dyke. Stephen prayed that they would not get caught and held by anything. The force of the current was keeping them down and Stephen had reached the point when he felt he had to open his mouth and draw in the water or burst his lungs when he found that the current was slackening and he could kick up towards the surface.

Gulping great lunguls of air and water, he struggled to hold Sarah's face above the surface. She made no movement and Stephen knew she was past struggling. A few strokes and he found he could touch the bottom. Half swimming, half wading and trying to keep the wind behind him, Stephen set off for, as he hoped, dry ground. Soon the water receded to his knees but there it seemed to stay. The marsh was so gently shelving that the combined floodwaters from river and sea had spread far inland. Sarah was now a dead weight in his arms and it took a tremendous effort to get her up over his shoulder. Somehow he had to get the water out of her lungs and he prayed that the movement of her head flopping against his back would effect this.

Stephen plodded on, only half aware of what he was doing. His leg was aching from the cold and Sarah's kick and the brackish water bit painfully into the raw skin of his burnt arm but all this was secondary to his dread that Sarah might be dead. Summoning all his remaining strength, he tried to go faster. It was a while before he realised that the only water round his feet was in his boots.

He dumped Sarah unceremoniously on the muddy ground, fighting the urge just to sink down beside her — the time to rest was not yet. He managed to unfasten his cloak and, spreading it out, he rolled Sarah face downwards onto it. He thought he could feel a faint heartbeat and, as he had done to Mistress Fuller, he began to move her arms and shoulders up and down, trying to get air back into her lungs. It was an eternity before she coughed and he could feel her ribs move of their own accord. Thankfully he could detect a stronger heartbeat but she was still only semi-conscious, as much, he supposed, from the shocking events of the night as from the near drowning. Kneeling in the mud, Stephen offered up a prayer of thanks for their escape.

Sarah needed warmth but for the moment he was too exhausted to carry her any further. Stephen sat down on the edge of his cloak, gathered Sarah into his lap and pulled the rest of the cloak up round them. Being wet, it did little to keep out the cold but it was better than nothing and it did keep the worst of the wind off them. He felt bitterly cold and he wished he had some means of warming Sarah. With everything soaked wet, a fire was impossible, so he could only hold her close and hope she would gain some warmth from his body.

He supposed he must have dozed off from sheer exhaustion, for the next thing he knew was Sarah screaming hysterically and struggling to escape from his encircling arms. Mindful of her previous attack, he grabbed her wrists. Her mind might still be deranged by shock.

"Whoa, love!" he said gently. "Calm

down! No one is going to hurt you now. You are quite safe!"

"Stephen?" she said questioningly, peering wildly up at him.

"Yes, love. Who else?"

"All I can see is a great black creature that looks like Death himself!"

Stephen pushed back his hair. "We did brush rather close to the gentleman!" he admitted mildly.

"George?"

"Dead." There was no point in dressing up the knowledge.

Sarah shuddered but her movement was towards Stephen now. Suddenly she was against his chest, sobbing — not wildly, but with a controlled hopelessness that betokened months of pent-up grief. The sound tore at Stephen's heart and, feeling totally inadequate, he could only hold her close and rock her like a child. She was not ready yet to be comforted. He knew they should be on their feet moving to keep warm but it would be dangerous to rush Sarah after all she had been through. There would be questions too that she was bound to ask and which he was in no hurry to answer.

At last her sobs died down to quiet little gulps and he began to chafe her hands.

"Stephen, I never meant to kill Sir George not when I started out tonight." She said wretchedly.

"Nor did you kill him, my love."

"What do you mean? I can remember him dropping his guard — he must have seen you — and I thrust at him . . . " She shuddered.

"Nevertheless you did not touch him. A Higher Authority took retribution before you could. Sir George was snatched off the wall by a wave and he must have died within seconds."

Sarah digested this in silence for a while, then she said stonily: "But the intent was there by then."

"No," he contradicted firmly. "You were just carried away by the heat of the moment, that is all. Besides I know perfectly well what you did intend to happen tonight."

She looked up at him quickly, trying to see his face in the darkness. "How can you know?"

"Because I am coming to know you

quite well, my love! You set out tonight not to kill, but to be killed, didn't you?"

She stiffened and Stephen felt her nod rather than heard her soft 'Yes'.

"It was like planning your own murder," he chided.

"It was the perfect solution — and it seemed the best way out for all of us."

Her words were tinged with regret and Stephen realised that Sarah had lived her revenge for so long that she had not yet absorbed the fact that Sir George had gone out of her life for ever. He had so dominated her thoughts that his evil lingered on.

"Death is never the best way out — though, I grant you, Sir George's death is a great blessing for us! You should have trusted me more — it would have given me great pleasure to have rid you of him!"

Sarah flung her arms round his neck. "Stephen! Oh, Stephen, I'm so sorry and ashamed! I was so obsessed that even though I knew I was hurting you I went right on doing it. It was like an all-consuming fire or a madness that came over me like a mist creeping off the marsh. You have heard people talk of marsh madness and certainly this marsh has been evil enough for all of us."

"With that I agree — so let us try to get away from it," he said briskly. "That is, love, unless you want to sink down into this stinking mud forever!" he added, as he pushed her off his lap and rose stiffly to his feet.

Sarah got up obediently and stood swaying slightly. Stephen looked around. It was lighter and the wind seemed less strong. Either the clouds had thinned, allowing more moonlight to filter through, or the dawn was approaching. He had lost all count of time and the watch in his pocket had stopped — probably forever.

"I wish I knew where we are exactly — this whole damned marsh looks alike to me!" he said aloud.

"Unless the wind has shifted we have only to walk with it behind us to reach the high ground," Sarah pointed out.

"I don't want the high ground — I want the river bank. I left Land-Lubber somewhere near the river when the flood waters got too deep for him to carry me further and riding strikes me as being a preferable method of transport to walking!"

"Maybe — but you'll be lucky if he is still there. The moment I dismounted, Star Lady bolted for home and Fanworth's mount did the same. They were both terrified by the storm."

"Land-Lubber is made of sterner stuff — I hope! The only time I have known him to be really nervous was during the fire tonight."

"Fire?"

"The windmill was burnt down. Didn't you know?"

"If you mean did I set fire to it — no, I didn't! The men easily could have, though. I have never known them to be in such an ugly mood — they certainly didn't need me to urge them on."

Stephen heaved an inward sigh of relief. The details of Johnnie's death were bizarre enough without any added complications. Holding Sarah close to his side and with his cloak still round both of them, Stephen began to guide her footsteps towards the river. As they reached the bank a shaft of moonlight shone through a rift in the clouds. Stephen was dismayed to see how low on the horizon the moon was — he wanted Sarah safely back at Banks House before the servants were about. The beam of light was quickly gone but before it disappeared Stephen had spotted his horse farther along the bank.

"Hurry, love!" he said urgently. "We must try and get you home before it gets light — by the moon it is nearly dawn."

"My wedding-day." Sarah said expressionlessly.

"No, my love. I don't think I can get hold of a Bishop's Licence that fast!" he said seriously.

"Cousin, are you offering for me?" Sarah stopped and looked up at him, a sudden grin lightening her face.

Stephen smiled at her childishly eager look. "It is hardly the time or the place — but if your ladyship will have me?"

"Oh, Stephen, can you doubt!" For the second time that night she flung her arms round him.

Great as was their need to hurry, Stephen stood still in his tracks and kissed her. Cold and time were forgotten as lips and tongues explored in mutual ecstasy and when they parted both felt as if they had been warmed by fire. Hands entwined, he drew her gently onward.

"Come, love, we have got to hurry. I mean to beg, borrow or steal your brother's coach and get you away before anyone comes to embarrass you with questions or sympathy about Fanworth's disappearance."

"Where are you going to take me?" Sarah sounded more tired than interested.

"To our Aunt and Uncle Perrington. Aunt Bess dearly wished to be at your wedding, remember? But first you are going to have a hot tub and some sleep."

Sarah's attention had wandered. Her steps dragged and again she halted.

"I still cannot marry you, Stephen," The dejected hopelessness was back in her voice.

"What do you mean?" he asked sharply. There was no time for a long argument.

"You forget my reason for marrying Sir George."

"Oh, no, I haven't! You promised your father to marry Fanworth in order to get Gerton Hall back for your brother, but Fanworth is dead and Thomas has his hall. Also your vowed revenge for John Carr's murder has been taken care of."

"You forget — what about Johnnie?"

Of course, Johnnie. He looked down at the mulish expression on her face and wondered what she had planned for the poor little mite if her plan had succeeded and Fanworth had killed her that night.

As if reading his thoughts, she answered him. "George would have taken care of him. With the scandal ensuing from my death he could hardly threaten Tom or Father O'Brien with him. Besides, his one soft spot was Johnnie — the child lacked nothing and he certainly was never ill-treated."

Stephen remembered the comfortable warm nursery and the contented child. Oh, Fanworth had taken the greatest care of Johnnie while the child was of use to him. Stephen had not the heart to tell Sarah of Farnworth's scheme to eliminate Johnnie even before his short span came to its natural conclusion.

Aloud he said firmly: "Johnnie never was your responsibility — he was Father O'Brien's son!"

"Was? Is?"

Stephen sighed. He had not wanted to tell Sarah about Johnnie's death until later — she had already suffered too many shocks for one night — but he could see there was no other way to move her.

"Sarah," he said quietly. "Johnnie is dead too."

"But he can't be! He was quite well this afternoon."

"I know but he must have seen the fire and decided to go to watch it. Somehow he escaped from the house and he died when part of the windmill collapsed on to him."

Her reaction was what he feared it might be.

"Then I killed him," she said dully. "I led the men in there tonight."

"Sarah, you mustn't take it like that. You didn't kill him — you didn't start the fire in the windmill. Besides there are too many other factors. If Fanworth hadn't told Johnnie he might watch the

Guy Fawkes Night bonfire or if his nurse had taken better care of him he would still be alive. Nobody thought of Johnnie when they lit that fire but he was happy when he died — he was smiling. This way he did not suffer, there was no time. It was over so quickly."

Sarah was crying again, but softly, and she did not reply. A moment later she allowed Stephen to lead her onwards again.

Land-Lubber was standing quietly on the now much diminished patch of dry ground. His head was drooping and he gave the appearance of snoozing placidly. They had nearly reached his side before he looked up.

Sarah giggled hysterically. "He must be the only one not disturbed by the night's events!" she gasped, half sobbing.

Stephen grinned crookedly. "You may take back all your past words of ridicule! I admit he is no racehorse but he is here and he will take the two of us with ease, which will save a long walk!"

He made to lift Sarah sideways onto the saddle but she twisted away from him.

"Give me a leg up, Stephen! I am wearing breeches, remember! I have a mind to ride astride for the last time, for no doubt you will be so starched as to forbid it when we are wed!"

Stephen's heart lifted. "Yes, my sweet — certainly I mean to play the heavy husband! There must be no more tomboy behaviour from my lady wife!" But, smiling, he obliged her.

Sarah waited until he was settled on Land-Lubber's broad back, his long legs dangling on either side.

"Stephen, I will promise never to be a hoyden again, if you will promise me one thing?"

"What might that be?"

"Please don't ever call me 'sweetheart'."

"No, my dearest love. I never will."

Stephen dug his knees into the horse's flanks and turned his head away from the marsh.

Other titles in the Ulverscroft Large Print Series:

TO FIGHT THE WILD
Rod Ansell and Rachel Percy

Lost in uncharted Australian bush, Rod Ansell survived by hunting and trapping wild animals, improvising shelter and using all the bushman's skills he knew.

COROMANDEL
Pat Barr

India in the 1830s is a hot, uncomfortable place, where the East India Company still rules. Amelia and her new husband find themselves caught up in the animosities which seethe between the old order and the new.

THE SMALL PARTY
Lillian Beckwith

A frightening journey to safety begins for Ruth and her small party as their island is caught up in the dangers of armed insurrection.

THE WILDERNESS WALK
Sheila Bishop

Stifling unpleasant memories of a misbegotten romance in Cleave with Lord Francis Aubrey, Lavinia goes on holiday there with her sister. The two women are thrust into a romantic intrigue involving none other than Lord Francis.

THE RELUCTANT GUEST
Rosalind Brett

Ann Calvert went to spend a month on a South African farm with Theo Borland and his sister. They both proved to be different from her first idea of them, and there was Storr Peterson — the most disturbing man she had ever met.

ONE ENCHANTED SUMMER
Anne Tedlock Brooks

A tale of mystery and romance and a girl who found both during one enchanted summer.

CLOUD OVER MALVERTON
Nancy Buckingham

Dulcie soon realises that something is seriously wrong at Malverton, and when violence strikes she is horrified to find herself under suspicion of murder.

AFTER THOUGHTS
Max Bygraves

The Cockney entertainer tells stories of his East End childhood, of his RAF days, and his post-war showbusiness successes and friendships with fellow comedians.

MOONLIGHT AND MARCH ROSES
D. Y. Cameron

Lynn's search to trace a missing girl takes her to Spain, where she meets Clive Hendon. While untangling the situation, she untangles her emotions and decides on her own future.

NURSE ALICE IN LOVE
Theresa Charles

Accepting the post of nurse to little Fernie Sherrod, Alice Everton could not guess at the romance, suspense and danger which lay ahead at the Sherrod's isolated estate.

POIROT INVESTIGATES
Agatha Christie

Two things bind these eleven stories together — the brilliance and uncanny skill of the diminutive Belgian detective, and the stupidity of his Watson-like partner, Captain Hastings.

LET LOOSE THE TIGERS
Josephine Cox

Queenie promised to find the long-lost son of the frail, elderly murderess, Hannah Jason. But her enquiries threatened to unlock the cage where crucial secrets had long been held captive.

THE TWILIGHT MAN
Frank Gruber

Jim Rand lives alone in the California desert awaiting death. Into his hermit existence comes a teenage girl who blows both his past and his brief future wide open.

DOG IN THE DARK
Gerald Hammond

Jim Cunningham breeds and trains gun dogs, and his antagonism towards the devotees of show spaniels earns him many enemies. So when one of them is found murdered, the police are on his doorstep within hours.

THE RED KNIGHT
Geoffrey Moxon

When he finds himself a pawn on the chessboard of international espionage with his family in constant danger, Guy Trent becomes embroiled in moves and countermoves which may mean life or death for Western scientists.

TIGER TIGER
Frank Ryan

A young man involved in drugs is found murdered. This is the first event which will draw Detective Inspector Sandy Woodings into a whirlpool of murder and deceit.

CAROLINE MINUSCULE
Andrew Taylor

Caroline Minuscule, a medieval script, is the first clue to the whereabouts of a cache of diamonds. The search becomes a deadly kind of fairy story in which several murders have an other-worldly quality.

LONG CHAIN OF DEATH
Sarah Wolf

During the Second World War four American teenagers from the same town join the Army together. Forty-two years later, the son of one of the soldiers realises that someone is systematically wiping out the families of the four men.

THE LISTERDALE MYSTERY
Agatha Christie

Twelve short stories ranging from the light-hearted to the macabre, diverse mysteries ingeniously and plausibly contrived and convincingly unravelled.

TO BE LOVED
Lynne Collins

Andrew married the woman he had always loved despite the knowledge that Sarah married him for reasons of her own. So much heartache could have been avoided if only he had known how vital it was to be loved.

ACCUSED NURSE
Jane Converse

Paula found herself accused of a crime which could cost her her job, her nurse's reputation, and even the man she loved, unless the truth came to light.

A GREAT DELIVERANCE
Elizabeth George

Into the web of old houses and secrets of Keldale Valley comes Scotland Yard Inspector Thomas Lynley and his assistant to solve a particularly savage murder.

'E' IS FOR EVIDENCE
Sue Grafton

Kinsey Millhone was bogged down on a warehouse fire claim. It came as something of a shock when she was accused of being on the take. She'd been set up. Now she had a new client — herself.

A FAMILY OUTING IN AFRICA
Charles Hampton and Janie Hampton

A tale of a young family's journey through Central Africa by bus, train, river boat, lorry, wooden bicyle and foot.

THE PLEASURES OF AGE
Robert Morley

The author, British stage and screen star, now eighty, is enjoying the pleasures of age. He has drawn on his experiences to write this witty, entertaining and informative book.

THE VINEGAR SEED
Maureen Peters

The first book in a trilogy which follows the exploits of two sisters who leave Ireland in 1861 to seek their fortune in England.

A VERY PAROCHIAL MURDER
John Wainwright

A mugging in the genteel seaside town turned to murder when the victim died. Then the body of a young tearaway is washed ashore and Detective Inspector Lyle is determined that a second killing will not go unpunished.

DEATH ON A HOT SUMMER NIGHT

Anne Infante

Micky Douglas is either accident-prone or someone is trying to kill him. He finds himself caught in a desperate race to save his ex-wife and others from a ruthless gang.

HOLD DOWN A SHADOW

Geoffrey Jenkins

Maluti Rider, with the help of four of the world's most wanted men, is determined to destroy the Katse Dam and release a killer flood.

THAT NICE MISS SMITH

Nigel Morland

A reconstruction and reassessment of the trial in 1857 of Madeleine Smith, who was acquitted by a verdict of Not Proven of poisoning her lover, Emile L'Angelier.

SEASONS OF MY LIFE
Hannah Hauxwell and Barry Cockcroft

The story of Hannah Hauxwell's struggle to survive on a desolate farm in the Yorkshire Dales with little money, no electricity and no running water.

TAKING OVER
Shirley Lowe and Angela Ince

A witty insight into what happens when women take over in the boardroom and their husbands take over chores, children and chickenpox.

AFTER MIDNIGHT STORIES, The Fourth Book Of

A collection of sixteen of the best of today's ghost stories, all different in style and approach but all combining to give the reader that special midnight shiver.

DEATH TRAIN
Robert Byrne

The tale of a freight train out of control and leaking a paralytic nerve gas that turns America's West into a scene of chemical catastrophe in which whole towns are rendered helpless.

THE ADVENTURE OF THE CHRISTMAS PUDDING
Agatha Christie

In the introduction to this short story collection the author wrote "This book of Christmas fare may be described as 'The Chef's Selection'. I am the Chef!"

RETURN TO BALANDRA
Grace Driver

Returning to her Caribbean island home, Suzanne looks forward to being with her parents again, but most of all she longs to see Wim van Branden, a coffee planter she has known all her life.

SKINWALKERS
Tony Hillerman

The peace of the land between the sacred mountains is shattered by three murders. Is a 'skinwalker', one who has rejected the harmony of the Navajo way, the murderer?

A PARTICULAR PLACE
Mary Hocking

How is Michael Hoath, newly arrived vicar of St. Hilary's, to meet the demands of his flock and his strained marriage? Further complications follow when he falls hopelessly in love with a married parishioner.

A MATTER OF MISCHIEF
Evelyn Hood

A saga of the weaving folk in 18th century Scotland. Physician Gavin Knox was desperately seeking a cure for the pox that ravaged the slums of Glasgow and Paisley, but his adored wife, Margaret, stood in the way.